THE BRIDGE

The Bridge

MANFRED GREGOR

translated by Robert S. Rosen

Random House
NEW YORK

THE BRIDGE

1

It was chance that, ten years later, led me back to the little town.

Or was it chance? As I stood on the bridge that evening and looked down into the river, I knew it was more my desire to return to the bridge that had brought me back. I stood on the wide pavement, leaning over the railing, looking down into the water, and turning from time to time to gaze at either bank.

It was a beautiful bridge and the little town could be proud of it. Its massive quarrystones stood firm against high tides. How thrilling, I recalled, to stand on the bridge in the spring when the river brought the melted snow down from the mountains! Sometimes a treetrunk, carried along by muddied yellow waters, thundered against the pilings; boiling foam, helpless against the strength of the bridge, surged about its foundations. On beautiful summer days it was a pleasure to watch the rowers come downstream, to see their tanned bodies in the racing boats.

But as I stood on the bridge this May evening, the river brought neither flood waters nor rowers. From the height of the bridge the water seemed shallow; one could see to the bottom. Near the center of the river bed lay a huge rock, left behind when the bridge was built in 1935. Just beyond the rock was a spot that had changed little in the decades since; there the broad back of the powerful stone prevented the deposit of debris, and the rifle lying on the gravelly bottom could still be seen. It was a 1944 sten gun. The magazine was empty.

The weapon had slipped out of a German soldier's hand on May 2nd, 1945, at 5:20 in the afternoon, had glided between the railings, caught at the magazine, and swung to and fro for about a second. Then the soldier collapsed, and, falling, pushed the rifle downward. The soldier had had his sixteenth birthday only a month earlier. As he collapsed, his lips moved as though they were forming the words of a prayer.

I knew that I would not forget him or the others.

It all began ten years before, in the barracks of this little German town. To be exact, on the first of May, 1945.

The river meandered gently through the center of the town, dividing it into two halves. The link was the massive bridge. The town lay in the midst of a magnificent landscape: wide woods, chains of hills, and dark-green meadows. Once two wanderers met on one of the hills overlooking the town.

"I'd like to be buried in a place like this!" one of them sighed. "Not I," the other said, taking a deep breath. "I'd like to live here!"

They had both meant the same thing.

2

Karl Horber had just stepped under the shower. The water was cold as ice, and he took care not to get it directly on his chest or his back. Gingerly he let it trickle down his narrow shoulders.

Further along the wall of the barracks washroom, below the half-open door, the Gang idled about. With mock interest they watched Horber as he tried to wash away the dirt that still clung to him from the field drill. They always had fun with Horber. He was called "Chop-chop" because on the day he had been assigned to lead the platoon in a detail Horber had added the words, "chop-chop!" to every command. Horber belonged to the Gang himself, and was well liked. With his protruding ears, freckled face, and flame-red hair, the lad of sixteen was used to ridicule.

He proved again, under the shower, that he could take it. For the Gang were not sparing with helpful hints.

"Just don't get your belly wet, Chop-chop, it might rust on you!"

"Put your ears back if you want to get some water on your neck!"

"It's a shame we can't have your girl watch you now. Man, how does she ever get enough looking at you!"

They roared with laughter after each remark, and immediately another member of the Gang tried to come up with an even funnier one. Karl Horber laughed too. Not because this was the best defense. He was so full of good cheer, he simply had to laugh at jokes, even jokes about himself.

Horber laughed, and his whole body—the lanky legs, the stomach, the convex back with its bony shoulders— seemed to shake with laughter. Then suddenly Schaubeck stood in the doorway; Sergeant Schaubeck, known as "The Beast."

Nobody knew who had given Schaubeck that name. Nobody ever thought it necessary to ask. Schaubeck had the reputation of being able to straighten out the most obstinate recruit, and no one ever questioned it. As long as he kept his mouth shut he seemed harmless enough. But there was something ominous about his voice, which always had a tinge of sarcasm. His voice sounded ominous even when, with exaggerated cheerfulness, he displayed his military knowledge; still more when he shouted, and most of all when he whispered.

"Horber," he whispered, "you slob. Can't you even wash yourself properly? Do you want me to send for your mother and have her wash your behind?"

Then louder. "Get under that shower, maaaarch!"

Horber stood motionless under the shower. Schaubeck turned the faucet as far as it would go. He was by no

6

means through with Horber when he heard a voice from the corner to which the Gang had withdrawn—low, but clearly audible, "Turn it off, you bastard!"

Quiet.

"Who was it?" Schaubeck screamed.

Silence.

Louder: "Who was it?"

Silence.

Schaubeck, very softly now, "I want to know which one of you it was, do you understand? Or I'll break you, so help me, I'll knock the shit out of you!"

Dead silence in the Gang. Suddenly the same voice as before: "Like hell you will, filthy bastard!"

A calm, deep voice, sounding a trifle bored. The Gang knew it was Ernst Scholten, the snob among them: keen musician, fanatical about Bach, shies away from girls. Had once been arrested for vandalism.

The Gang was proud of Scholten, but at the same time a little afraid of him. He was, at sixteen, mature for his age, and capable of doing things that other boys of his class did not even dare think about.

Now, as always, the Gang was in the dark about Scholten's real motives. Agreed, Schaubeck was tormenting Horber—but was a little water going to kill him? Why pick a fight with Schaubeck over a thing like that? The Gang did not immediately realize that Scholten had reached the critical point, that he was simply fed up. None of the others had felt the mistreatment of the past fourteen days as painfully as he had. It had begun the very first time he found himself face to face with Schaubeck.

"What's your name?" he had been asked.

"Scholten." Then, after a moment's hesitation: "Ernst —Ernst Scholten."

7

Schaubeck, surprised: "Scholten? What a name! First time I've heard it. Brother, how can anyone be named Scholten?"

Schaubeck loved these little jokes and usually waited for the laughter that followed. But the six who stood around him and Scholten had not yet learned when Schaubeck expected them to laugh, and had remained silent.

Schaubeck continued: "Ever hear anything about civilization, Scholten?"

"Yes, sir!"

"Yes, sir! That's *yessir,* you slob, wake up! And the haircut is also part of our civilization. It is one of the achievements of civilization, wouldn't you say so?"

"Yes, sir!"

"Get going, you, have that jungle cleared! Let them take it all off. Dismissed!"

Ernst Scholten's haircut was indeed a far cry from standard army regulations, but he was simply not used to being told when he should go to the barber. And so, when he sat in the barber's stool an hour later he felt every snip of the clippers as a personal humiliation. This, with a host of other petty annoyances accumulated in the past two weeks, was now like a charge of dynamite behind every sentence Scholten hurled at his Sergeant from a safe cover.

An unusually tense atmosphere. Karl Horber trembling, naked and unhappy under the still running shower, clutching his thighs. With his back to him Schaubeck, cold rage in his heart, his face turned to the six lurking in the corner. The Gang—Walter Forst, Siegi Bernhard, Albert Mutz, Jürgen Borchart, Klaus Hager, and Scholten—were quietly waiting.

8

The five around Scholten were somewhat slow to follow. They began to sense, however, that there was more to this than one of "Winnetou's" usual pranks.

Scholten had come by this Indian nickname a long time ago. His jet-black hair, his lean, yellowish face with the sharply protruding nose and chin had something warlike about them. There were some people who formed an intense dislike for Scholten the first moment they saw him. Schaubeck was one of them. What next, the Gang wondered. How was this little scene going to end?

Just as Schaubeck stared them down, one after another, as though he could detect the one who had spoken out, the siren sounded.

Air-raid alarm.

Schaubeck whispered: "We'll have more to say about this later," and marched off.

NONCOM SCHAUBECK AND WHISKEY

Born in 1903. First name: Alois. Full name: Alois Schaubeck. Professional soldier. Specialist in the handling of men and equipment, women and whiskey. No stress on quality in women or in whiskey. Just let there be lots of both, and if possible even more. His idea of a great time: any night off duty.

There was some story in connection with Schaubeck. . . . What was it again? Ah, yes, Schaubeck had married. In a hurry. He had known Kitty only four or five days: "Look here, honey, Kitty is a sweet enough name, but you don't want to be called that, do you? Let's make it Cathy, agreed?"

War marriage.

9

Lasted all of four weeks. Then Schaubeck stopped coming home. Kitty went back to her work and Schaubeck to his women and whiskey. Occasionally he showed up at the saloon where Kitty worked, and from time to time he threw glances at her from the table where he sat with one of his buddies. After the second or third bottle of wine, Schaubeck was likely to say: "See that redhead over there, behind the bar? That's Kitty, I want you to know. Used to be my wife one time. Man, if you only knew! Quite a story. Had some wild times together, hahaha!" Then Schaubeck laughed. Boisterous and loud. And then he drank some more. And when he had had enough to drink, he displayed his knowledge of literature: "Say d'yuh know this one? . . . There once was a hostess in . . . Hahahaha, hahahaha!"

But there was more to Schaubeck's story. The portrait would be incomplete if we failed to mention that Schaubeck's platoon was in tiptop shape. That his superiors did not respect him, but that they valued the success of his methods. That no one could hit the dirt as quickly as one who had trained under Schaubeck.

Schaubeck spent the war in the homeland. Sometimes he bragged of a wound, but occasionally had the misfortune to be overheard by someone who knew better: "Don't shoot your mouth off, Schaubeck, or you'll get wounded again!" Again! Schaubeck had merely been injured in a traffic accident. But Ernst Scholten did not know that.

*

The seven boys raced from the shower-room to the anti-aircraft batteries, Karl Horber wearing only fatigues and a steel helmet. They hauled ammunition.

The anti-aircraft guns went into action, and the enemy bombers flew off, soaring high in the night sky. Only one American Mustang left its squadron, nose-dived across the barracks, and strafed the N.C.O. lounge as it zoomed past.

Two noncoms sat there playing cards, sharing a bottle of wine which one of them had managed to steal. Schaubeck had just finished telling Sergeant Heilmann about Karl Horber and the shower-room incident. Heilmann was not at all amused, and was just about to say that he hated to see the boys tortured for no reason at all, when he happened to glance at the ceiling.

Sergeant Heilmann froze.

It all happened with lightning speed, yet none of it escaped his notice. First, the holes on the ceiling. Marching forward in a straight line, they seemed to come directly towards him—and he pushed away from the table.

He threw himself down, to the right.

Plaster came down on top of him, he heard a crash—then it was over. When Heilmann got up again, he saw Schaubeck leaned across the table in a peculiarly twisted position; there were red splashes all over him. Red wine and blood.

Schaubeck's wide-open eyes were astonished.

His hands were clenched into fists.

3

The whole Gang was in the room when Lieutenant Fröhlich came in later. Horber made the report. After that Fröhlich stepped up to the first locker and said to them:

"Boys, Schaubeck is dead. The Amis are only twenty miles away from here. Everything has gone *kaput*. I'd like to see you beat it. Now. You understand that I am not in a position to issue an order to that effect. But I have told the post at the western wall. You can get through there."

This was all Fröhlich said. Then he looked so long and hard at each of them that it made them uncomfortable. And then he used language which no one had ever heard him use before. "Damn shit—war!"

It was only a mutter, like that of a man who is desperately trying to keep from weeping. But they had all heard it.

Fröhlich did an about-face, as if on parade ground, and left the room.

Two hours before the alarm he had received the news that the Russians had completely wiped out the German unit to which his son had been attached for the last three months.

The seven boys were devoted to Lieutenant Fröhlich. Aside from Sergeant Heilmann, he alone concerned himself about their welfare. The Gang felt lost in the huge barracks; they were the last contingent from the little town.

They had been called away from their classroom in the middle of April, in a final mass conscription, had been fitted with field-gray uniforms and been issued new carbines. Schaubeck had welcomed them.

"Christ, look at that weary gang!"

Then cheerfully: "Well, the war won't be over that soon. There will still be time enough to make men out of you slobs!"

Ever since, they had been known in the barracks as the Gang. They themselves had boasted of the name "weary Gang" for so long that it finally stuck, and sometimes even appeared in official orders.

Then Schaubeck took over their basic training in his usual fashion. Aside from him, only Lieutenant Fröhlich and Sergeant Heilmann still bothered about them in the catastrophic confusion which prevailed in the barracks during the final days of the war. Fröhlich engaged them in long conversations about their homes and families, while Heilmann confined himself to making gloomy and ominous, albeit well-meant, prophecies in passing.

"Clear out, kids." Or: "Listen to me, boys, things are going from bad to worse. Pack up. Go back home to mother!"

They liked Heilmann, even though he seldom laughed or told jokes, and had a way of looking past them when he talked to them, as though he saw disaster looming in the distance.

But they loved Fröhlich, and that evening, when he told them of Schaubeck's death, felt an instinctive compassion for him. Franz Fröhlich, even in the uniform of a Lieutenant, hardly corresponded to the image of a German officer which a sixteen-year-old still retained in the spring of 1945.

LIEUTENANT FRÖHLICH AND JULIUS CAESAR

Lieutenant Fröhlich was not a career officer. He was a schoolteacher. He had enjoyed lecturing on Julius Caesar's wars and the strategy employed in them. The strategy of the Second World War gave him little joy. Nothing, in fact, did since he had left the school and the boys behind. And they had even drafted his son. He could not understand that. Flori was so little; he still played with trains—and with soldiers. Yes, even soldiers.

They still played together. The teacher was building trenches, walls and castles for his son, and explaining the strategy to him.

And in the midst of all that Florian Fröhlich was called away to the service.

The last time Franz Fröhlich saw his son, the boy wore a uniform with sleeves much too long, and a field cap behind which his lean face appeared even more delicate.

Then the seven boys came into the barracks. Fröhlich once happened to come by just as Schaubeck was engaged in making men out of the weary Gang. Schaubeck made Mutz do deep knee-bends with the carbine in hand.

Schaubeck counted: "Thirty-three, thirty-four, thirty-five—come on, you slob, don't fall asleep now, pull yourself together—thirty-six, thirty-seven . . ."

Suddenly Fröhlich saw his own son in place of the blond, ruddy Mutz. Saw him pant and gasp. "Bend your knees, stretch, bend your knees, stretch."

Fröhlich ordered Schaubeck to step forward and bawled him out—really let him have it.

What was Fröhlich left with? He still had a wife back home from whom he had become estranged over the years. He had a closet full of books, mostly on strategy—Julius Caesar and others. He had his lieutenant's uniform. He no longer had a school. Nor any students. Not even a son.

Only the seven boys in the barracks.

He thought: It is up to me to look after them. Take care, Fröhlich! They are your responsibility!

4

The alarm came in the middle of the night. The whistles blew shrilly. It was all exactly as they had practiced it.

The whistles tore most men from their sleep, but the seven boys were still wide awake when the alarm was sounded.

They had not been able to fall asleep after Fröhlich's talk, and stayed up arguing late into the night. Should they clear out? Should they take Fröhlich's hint and make off across the western wall? They had seldom been so much at odds as on this evening.

Karl Horber was all for leaving. (Scholten: "Go on, beat it, but chop-chop!" They roared with laughter.) Klaus Hager, nicknamed "the silent one," made a speech, his first in days. Sometimes one could not get him to open his mouth for hours. "Fellows, if we leave now, we are deserters, and deserters are shot. If we stay, we might also get killed. Still, I think it is safer to stay. We can always leave later."

That was typical of Hager. He always thought first before speaking. He was not always right, but you knew he had given what he said careful consideration. Albert Mutz grumbled about the abominable food; he wanted to be home again, in the little house on the outskirts of the town. There was even a chance he could hide them all there. Ernst Scholten, for the time being, refrained from expressing an opinion. Lying in bed (the upper bunk of course—because of the better air higher up, he explained), he merely threw in his cynical comments, and seemed content with the laughter they provoked.

Walter Forst was for staying: "Take it from me, this is going to get damn interesting!"

Scholten: "Sure, pal, any minute now we will start playing Cowboys and Indians!"

Siegi Bernhard: "I don't care one way or the other, I'll go along with whatever you decide."

Jürgen Borchart: "I'm not going to get myself killed here. I'm skipping out, right now!"

The way he had said it would have left little doubt in anyone's mind that he meant to do just that. Unless one happened to know Jürgen, as the Gang did. Jürgen wasn't going to leave any sooner than the rest. He always expressed firm convictions and then failed to act on them. All but one had now stated their opinions, and they were anxious to hear from him.

Karl Horber sat up in bed, theatrically sawed the air with his hands and declaimed: "Friends, stable-comrades, let us listen to the words of our wise chief; Winnetou shall decide!"

This gave Scholten an opening. He started to speak without raising himself from his bed, addressing the white-washed ceiling overhead as though he were alone in the room.

"If Fröhlich suggests that we leave, he must have a good reason—he means well. Strictly speaking, it was almost a command by a superior officer. That is, if we are going to be technical about it. And he knows what he is talking about—he has lots of experience. Unlike us, who have no experience. Or only a little.

"The question then boils down to this: shall we beat it because Fröhlich has experience, or stay on because we don't have any? Most of your arguments are ridiculous and only make me laugh. But there is something to what Forst said. It is going to be interesting all right. It sure as hell is.

"It still remains to be seen if it's going to get *too* interesting. I think of Schaubeck. We know what happened to him. Then again, if we are on our toes, we can stick around and wait for some action, and skip out later when the going gets too rough. Anyway—if we left now, we'd be cowards, wouldn't we?"

As if the thought that he would be a coward if he deserted had only just occurred to him, he shot up in bed, looked triumphantly about and shouted:

"Listen, guys, we're cowards if we leave now. Miserable cowards. They must want something from us. They are training us for a reason. They did not give us uniforms and rifles to desert with. Fellows, they need us now!"

And then condescendingly: "You can do as you please, I am staying. Winnetou will hold the fort; he owes that to his red brothers. Ugh, I have spoken."

Horber hardly let him finish. He hung suspended like a monkey from the upper bunk. His flame-red hair and protruding ears extended over the rim of the bed, and he screamed at Scholten: "You say that again, say I am a coward just one more time and I'll throw you out of the window!"

Scholten laughed in his face, and while Mutz and Borchart tickled Horber's feet, Scholten tapped him on the nose with his heel so that Horber had to let go of the bed and landed on the floor.

At once a free-for-all started down below. Scholten swung his legs over the side of his bed and let himself fall down on top of the brawling Gang. Frenzied screams, laughter, a banging of tables and chairs, till way past midnight. It was then that the alarm came.

The brawl stopped at once. They listened to the whistles. It was no mistake, they could hear it clearly now. They rushed to their lockers, pulled out full marching equipment, and dressed in feverish haste. The packs were ready. They just threw them over their shoulders. They fastened the swordbelts, bayonets, spades, cartridge-pouches, put steel helmets on their heads, slung the gasmasks around their necks, and raced out into the hall. They snatched the carbines out of the rifle cases as they passed, and their heavy boots went *trapp-trapp-trapp-trapp* down the stone steps. Outside, in the center court of the barracks square, the boys attached themselves to the Second Squad. Lieutenant Fröhlich's squad.

The companies lined up four deep. A gray jeep approached through the archway of the western wing. Three men got out.

"Some big brass," Scholten whispered. The company —and battalion—commanders were summoned to a conference. The soldiers, some five hundred men, were kept waiting outside, lined up in roll-call formation.

Half an hour later the troopleaders emerged. Then

the commands echoed across the square, and one formation after another got under way. Lieutenant Fröhlich, Sergeant Heilmann and Corporal Wehnelt advanced with the Second Squad to the gymnasium, the seven boys trailing behind. In front of the gymnasium the squad formed a half-circle around their Lieutenant.

"The Americans are only twenty miles outside the town. It has been decided to . . . to put up a defense." It was with enormous reluctance that Fröhlich got past the last sentence.

"We will now take up positions that are essential to the defense of the town, positions we will have to hold."

He lost the thread of what he was saying, and his glance strayed over towards the seven boys at the left flank as though he expected them to come to his aid.

"We have to cover an extensive area with relatively few men. Now take up heavy arms, bazookas, ammunition—also iron rations!" Abruptly Fröhlich turned about and trudged off to the gymnasium.

Corporal Wehnelt bellowed: "Break step—maaaaarch!"

The squad numbered forty-two men. Each of them took two bazookas. Then they lined up for the sten guns. When Heilmann reached the Gang at the end of the line, he asked: "Any of you boys know how to handle one of these?"

"I do," Scholten said, as nonchalantly as if he had been asked whether he knew Mark Antony's funeral oration. The Gang was not surprised.

They were getting used to the idea that Scholten knew just about everything. Why shouldn't he know how to fire a sten?

Horber was given a Russian semi-automatic rifle. (Scholten: "He can't even shoot an ordinary carbine without making in his pants!") The rest of the Gang held onto their carbines. A case of ammunition was placed on the table and each took as many clips as he had room for in his pockets.

The squad of forty-two men climbed aboard two trucks. In three minutes they reached the bridge, where Fröhlich ordered them to halt. Sergeant Heilmann got off and called: "What's keeping our weary Gang?"

Disgruntled, the seven jumped off the platform of the truck to the street. Lieutenant Fröhlich: "The bridge is of strategic importance. You are to hold it. Sergeant Heilmann will be in charge." Then he said softly to Heilmann: "As soon as the fun starts, you clear out. Is that clear? I am holding you personally responsible for that."

They saw Heilmann's face light up in a smile for the first time in the fourteen days they had known him. The smile spread across his features, took hold of every wrinkle and line in his craggy face, and he said: "Yes, sir! perfectly clear."

NONCOM HEILMANN AND THE WAR

Within three days they had a name for cadet Heilmann at the academy. They called him Johnny-Come-Lately. He was then about ten years older than the rest of the cadets in his class, but his slow way of speaking, the calm he radiated, made him appear even older. He gave his training officers no cause for censure and none for special praise. Then, with only four days left in the semester, something happened.

The Nazi officer in charge of political indoctrination

asked him if it were possible for a German who was not a staunch supporter of the regime to be a good officer. The question seemed so childishly simple that Heilmann for once was able to blurt his answer into the room without hesitating first: "Of course, *Herr Oberleutnant!*"

At the end of the semester, when three hundred newly commissioned officers went home on furlough, Heilmann traveled east. Back to his unit. Still a noncom.

The reason was not clear to him at first. It always took Heilmann considerable time to arrange things in a logical pattern, to think matters through. "Adolf Heilmann, you'd think the name alone predestined him for leadership," the company commander said, grinning, when he saw the pile of negative reports come to his desk. Heilmann, with some delay, sauntered in a few days after them. "How did you manage it, Heilmann?" the commander said to him. "You did it this time!" Heilmann listened without moving a muscle in his face. Only his eyes laughed.

On May 2nd, 1944, there was an attack against some Russian rear positions, which were being defended doggedly. The attack was repulsed. Adolf Heilmann was among those missing. Nobody knew what happened to him. Nobody had seen him. Heilmann was gone.

But that same night, the sentry of a neighboring unit was frightened out of his wits when the stillness around him was suddenly pierced by a rattling, dragging sound. As it crept closer, he lost his nerve. Forgot all about the automatic rifle, the hand-grenades—everything. He couldn't think any longer, was terrified by this monster making straight for him, and sounded the alarm, screaming: "The Ivans!" And then once again: "The Ivans!"

Startled by the sound of his own voice, the sentry pressed his back against the crumbling wall of his foxhole and stared out into the night. To the left and right of him, his comrades stumbled into ditches and holes, gasping breathlessly. Quite, quite close now, he heard a voice: "Shut up, you idiot, or I'll punch you in the nose."

A big, massive gray hulk dragged itself forward the last few yards to the German position, slid headlong into the ditch and lay there.

The following morning the news was relayed to Heilmann's company that Heilmann was no longer missing. Heavily wounded, he had dragged himself back to his own lines with nearly superhuman tenacity. He covered a distance of some several thousand yards, crawling on his stomach.

*

And now Heilmann stood on the bridge with seven boys of sixteen. The truck with Fröhlich and the remaining squad moved on, heading west towards the Americans. The knowledge that he was now responsible for the seven boys weighed heavily on Sergeant Heilmann.

5

I must do something now, Heilmann thought, I must keep them occupied or else they will get nervous. But nothing, absolutely nothing, occurred to him. And he said to Scholten, because he stood nearest him: "Now we will just have to wait and see what happens! Scholten, usually so reserved and mature, made a wry face and without any show of respect asked: "Why the hell did they have to leave us behind here? Now we are going to miss everything again, just when it starts to get interesting!"

Heilmann said wearily: "Let's wait and see. It will get interesting enough right here too."

It did by and by. Few civilians still crossed the bridge at this late hour. Several columns drove by, heading west to meet the Americans. Then nothing stirred. The seven leaned against the railing; Heilmann walked back and forth.

How stupid of me, he thought, not to know what to do with them. Down below, the water rippled over pebbles and stones. The river was at work, ceaselessly carrying stones and sand along its journey. After a long rain it swelled into a mighty stream, but in dry summers it dwindled to a rill. One could easily wade across it then. The boys had once written a composition: "The River —a Symbol of Our Town." Horber had given a long, graphic description of the river: the green waters, the dipping willow trees along the banks. He expanded on the theme along these lines, and got an "A" easily enough.

Scholten failed to get a passing mark. "Missed the point," ran the comment across his paper. He had made the mistake of letting the river speak like a man, and was forced to the conclusion that this approach did not meet everyone's approval.

In the middle of the night, the retreat from the west set in. Heilmann's group was squatting close together at the eastern end of the bridge when a stream of columns flooded across: trucks, horse-drawn vehicles, cannons, a tank every now and then. In between came the men —weary, exhausted, staggering figures in mud-smeared uniforms—their hollow-cheeked faces, pale and unshaven, their necks bowed as though they felt a ghost sitting over them tirelessly cracking a whip. From time to time one of the men called over to the cowering boys: "What are you waiting for? Why don't you beat it!" Embarrassed, the boys turned their faces away and stared down into the river. And Heilmann cursed himself for a fool, because he still did not know what to do.

It began to rain lightly. The eight men on the bridge unbuckled the tarpaulins from their packs. Shivering, they draped the coarse material around themselves. As the columns continued to pass, it seemed to the boys that every marching step they heard carried them closer to the greatest event of their lives.

They were afraid. Not one of the seven would have owned up to it just then. But it was so.

They smoked; Heilmann had generously distributed cigarettes. They stuck them between their lips, struck matches to them with numb fingers, then sucked in the smoke with deep, hasty draughts. Only Albert Mutz coughed; he always coughed when he smoked. The other boys were used to cigarettes by now.

As the night wore on, the line of columns thinned and broke completely every now and then. After a while more vehicles rolled past, and beneath their rain-heavy tarpaulins lay combat-weary foot soldiers. And so it went. Vehicles—nothing. Vehicles—nothing.

And then the column ended. That was eerie, frightening; there had been a continuous stream—of carts, of trucks laden with men. Now suddenly, the seven were alone on the bridge with their sergeant. Heilmann thought and brooded.

He was almost grateful when he saw a jeep racing down the bridge ramp. With screeching brakes it came to a halt near the little group. Heilmann walked over to the jeep, looking forward to a chat with some staff driver. He was startled when he saw a full General before him. The General rose from his seat in the rear of the jeep, and with a sprightly movement jumped down to the pavement.

"Sergeant Heilmann with seven men on bridge patrol," Heilmann reported. He could not think of anything more sensible to say.

The General obviously no longer put much emphasis on form. Intentionally he overlooked the boys who

26

stumbled forward with the tarpaulins hanging loosely around their shoulders. In low, insistent tones, he kept on at Heilmann.

The boys could only hear their Sergeant.

"Yes, *Herr General!*"

"No, *Herr General!*"

"Very good, *Herr General!*"

The General spoke loud enough then, so that the seven could hear him as well: "I expect the bridge to be held, come what may. Do you understand? Under all circumstances. I'll see to it that you get some reinforcements!"

And as quickly as he had come, the General was off.

For a moment Heilmann thought he had been dreaming it all, but Borchart brought him back to harsh reality: "Was that a real General, Sergeant?"

"Yes, that was a General all right," Heilmann said fiercely, and let loose a blast of filthy, vulgar curses.

But the curses brought him no relief. I just wonder what those reinforcements are going to look like, Heilmann thought. I really wonder.

As it was, he did not have to wait long for them. A truck came into view. Like the jeep earlier, it came down the bridge ramp. The truck discharged eight, nine, ten figures in gray uniforms. Heilmann walked up to them, took one close look, and said: "Jesus Christ!"

That was all he said.

The reinforcement consisted of ten old men, all over sixty. Obviously drummed together in the last few hours, torn away from their homes, their kitchen tables. They had not been wearing these uniforms very long. Not that it mattered—the uniforms had proved themselves. They were torn and patched. The men who had formerly worn them were dead, fallen somewhere in France or Russia. They had been stripped of their coats when their riddled bodies were put on the operating tables. The coats could be patched again.

The ten old men had been given the same order as the seven boys; they had received it in silence. The old and the young alike. They had accepted the command as one accepts a report card at the end of the school year.

Heilmann was still brooding. He felt that he ought to do something, but did not know what.

The eighteen on the bridge had rifles, bazookas, ammunition, and iron rations. The iron ration consisted of a tin of blood sausage, a tin of beef, and Zwieback. They had taken the tins as they had taken the bazookas. One in the left hand, one in the right.

It doesn't make sense, Heilmann thought, to put men of sixty and boys of sixteen together like this on a bridge, and expect them to carry out an order. Their feelings about military orders and the war in general are bound to be poles apart. And not one of these people knows how to defend a bridge.

To be quite honest, Heilmann said to himself, I don't know either. But I do know one can't hold a bridge by just standing around on it. One would have to take up a central position from which the entire bridge can be controlled. The question is where? And how? And one would need a machine gun for that.

Here was an inspiration at last. Something to be done. Of course—a machine gun.

"Borchart, Mutz, Horber, hurry over to the barracks and tell them to send us a machine gun. A light machine gun and ammunition. Lots of ammunition, do you understand?"

The three said they understood, and left, visibly

glad to escape this waiting around, at least for an hour.

The old men stood together in a group and conversed in whispers, as though one loud word could bring about some disaster. Suddenly one of them did speak up, a man with sparse, silver-gray hair and a thin voice: "This is the end, you hear, the end!"

He had addressed no one in particular. He had spoken into the night. Then he looked sideways at Heilmann.

Heilmann did not reply. The old man pulled a watch out of his pocket. It was an old-fashioned watch with a cover that snapped open when pressed. Possibly a confirmation present. As if this confirmation watch had given him some sort of advice, he snapped to attention and said: "I'm going home!"

Nobody objected, although the old man waited a while.

"The order to hold the bridge cannot be carried out," he said. And again, after a brief pause: "I'm going."

He spoke with undue emphasis, very softly. Then he carefully leaned his carbine against the stone rampart, and walked away with quick, short steps.

This was the beginning. The old men, one after another, put their weapons down and left. At the end there were ten rifles leaning against the stone enclosure of the bridge and a pile of bazookas lying on the ground. The iron rations were all they had taken with them.

Sergeant Heilmann watched the departure of the ten men without batting an eyelash. Straddle-legged, his arms folded behind his back, he stood there and watched. He was helpless. *You've got to do something, Heilmann. You can't just let them go off. This is mutiny!* These thoughts raced through his brain, but Heilmann did not lift a finger.

When the last of the ten had gone, Heilmann turned

to face the boys. He was surprised to note with how much fervor and respect they looked up to him. They looked as though they were only waiting for him to issue an order now to carry it out at once. Heilmann had become a hero in their eyes. Precisely because he had let the men go. Let him rely on the boys. They wouldn't let him down. Mutz, Borchart and Horber returned on a truck. They unloaded two machine guns and several cases of ammunition. The truck rumbled off again.

"They didn't want to give us anything at first," Horber bragged, "so we went straight to the General."

"Well done," Heilmann acknowledged without much enthusiasm. He asked the boys about the situation in the barracks, and whether they had noticed anything as they came through the older sections of the town. Heilmann made a mental note of the fact that the boys had encountered no M.P.'s along the way. There would be no danger, he concluded, if one had to suddenly clear out. Then he assembled the machine guns, right in the middle of the street. He explained the parts to them as he went along. In much the same manner he had explained the workings of the machine gun, before new recruits, at least a thousand times. He stopped abruptly. A little more and he would have told them how to clean a machine gun—as if these two guns would ever be cleaned again.

Morning dawned in the east. Heilmann had come to the end of his instruction. There was little he could add to the theory of it, and as for the practice—well, he'd spare the boys that. Heilmann suddenly remembered Fröhlich. I wonder where he is now? And then he remembered Fröhlich's charge: "As soon as the fun starts here, you clear out. I am holding you personally responsible for that, Heilmann!"

Heilmann's deliberations had come to an end. He knew what to do at last. And why postpone any longer what was inevitable?

"Listen, boys," he said, "none of this makes sense. Your parents are waiting for you at home, and here you are wanting to play war. I promised Lieutenant Fröhlich not to let it come to that. You must help me to keep my promise!"

Heilmann had seldom made so long and carefully planned a speech. He was visibly proud of it. To keep the boys from thinking of a reply and raising objections, he went on: "I'm going off now for a little stroll around town. To see if the air is clear. I'll be back in ten minutes, and off we go then. To Kassel. No one is to leave before I get back, is that clear? And then we'll skip out together, in style. That too can be quite an experience!"

Heilmann rummaged about in his pack, and pulled out a civilian jacket, which he put on over his uniform, proving that in spite of his mental slowness Heilmann was not unprepared for a turn of events. But even so, he had miscalculated.

He had crossed the intersection near the bridge and proceeded up the street only a few yards when a pair of boots stamped out of a courtyard he was about to pass. Two unmoving faces stared at him from below the sharp rim of steel helmets. A pair of metal badges gleamed up at him.

M.P.'s, thought Heilmann. It's all over.

He showed them his papers, as he was asked to.

"Why the civilian jacket?" one of the two asked with a dour expression. "Knocking off a little too soon, aren't we?" the other M.P. said.

Heilmann walked between the two and feverishly worked his brain. He wasn't overly concerned with saving his own skin now. He only thought of the boys back on the bridge. He racked his brain: Christ, how can I make them understand? What can I do? I must do something . . . I must do something!

His fist landed on the nose of one of the M.P.'s. He brought his knee up and kicked him in the stomach, as hard as he could. But he couldn't get the right grip on the second one, and had only one alternative: to run, to run for dear life.

The first bullet from the .45 whistled past him, ricocheted off the wall of the building and smashed into the plaster. Heilmann jumped from side to side.

I must look like a rabbit, like a rabbit. He felt a blow against his back. He wanted to run on, but suddenly his legs gave way under him. Full length, he hit the pavement. Twice he tried, with all the strength still left him, to raise himself up on his elbows. Then Sergeant Heilmann was dead.

The M.P. found in the Sergeant's wallet his identification papers, a paybook and fifty-eight marks, a silver medallion of the Madonna, and a snapshot of a girl in a bathing suit. He slipped the wallet with papers and medallion into the pocket of his long coat. Then he looked at the snapshot by the light of his cigarette lighter.

"Nice babe," the M.P. said. Only then did he go to look after his comrade, who was cowering against the wall, groaning, his arms clasped around his stomach.

On the bridge, the seven boys waited for their Sergeant.

6

"I hear shooting," Horber said. They strained to hear. But after two muffled sounds there were no more.

"Perhaps somebody committed suicide," big Mutz whispered, and a shudder ran down his spine. "Sheer nonsense," Scholten said. He actually felt as miserable as the rest. Damn it all, if only Heilmann would come back.

What a ghastly feeling it was to be deserted on the bridge, to sit and wait. The day came on gradually; light poured in from the hills in the east. The rain had subsided a little.

"Suppose Heilmann leaves us in the lurch . . . ?" Mutz muttered.

"He won't leave you in the lurch, big sissy!"

Scholten can get nasty at times, Mutz thought. (I can still express an opinion, after all!)

And as it was, Heilmann did leave them in the lurch. The ten minutes turned into two hours. The seven began to argue again: had Heilmann deserted, or had he been forcibly detained someplace?

They stopped arguing at last. There was no sense to it, since no one could know for certain. Nor was it so terribly important. It had become a lot lighter meanwhile, and everything assumed a brighter aspect in daylight. Horber brought a little life into the Gang.

"Hey, we forgot our breakfast!" Everyone laughed. They watched Horber attack his tin of sausage with the bayonet. Twice it slipped, and once he pricked his finger.

"Get me to a hospital, quick, I'm bleeding to death!"

They roared with laughter; they were as wild as on a school hike. The din of a motor arose. Scholten listened: "Be quiet a moment!"

They all stopped to listen; the school-hike mood had vanished.

The sound did not come from the west, but came from the older part of the town. Once again a jeep raced down the bridge ramp as it had done earlier in the night and stopped with screeching brakes. It was the General. Up front this time, next to the driver. Two more soldiers sat in the rear.

The seven jumped to their feet, and snapped to attention as well as they could. Scholten stammered through the report. His face had turned crimson.

The General interrupted with a gesture of his hand: "Where is your noncom?"

Scholten remained silent, but Mutz, overly eager, said: "He's gone, General!"

He realized almost immediately that he was snitching on Heilmann (Christ, the Gang would never forgive him that!) and had the presence of mind to add: "He went to see about more ammunition for us!"

Brazenly, unabashed, he had lied. Suddenly it struck

Mutz: That's a General you're lying to, no good can come of that.

The General was curt and to the point: "How long is he gone?"

Mutz paled. "Two hours, General!" The General considered this. It seemed to Mutz now that in this attitude the General bore a resemblance to Napoleon as he appeared in a picture in his history book. Only the forelock was missing. The General was still considering when a grin flitted across his face, quite suddenly, and was gone.

He turned around in the jeep: "Schlopke!"

"Yes sir, General?"

The man in the rear left of the jeep snapped to attention in a sitting position, his whole face assuming an air of alertness.

"Get off, Schlopke. You're going to take over the show here!" Again the grin on the General's face: "We do want to get into this war a little before it is all over, Schlopke, don't we?!"

"*Yessir,* General!" Schlopke replied with zeal, and thought to himself: You know what you can do.

He jumped out of the jeep, and landed on the pavement with the resilience of a trained athlete.

"You are to hold the bridge, Schlopke, do you understand?"

The General had spoken softly. In a louder voice he added: "You've got seven splendid chaps here. A few thousand more like them and we might still win the war, Schlopke."

The boys blushed with pride and excitement. Of course they'd hold the bridge. They even had a noncom again. So it wasn't Heilmann. So his name was Schlopke.

But hadn't he come straight from the General's jeep?

"Do your stuff, boys. I'm relying on you," the General said, and drove off.

Schlopke called softly after the departing jeep: "Getting sick in the brain, or something, in your old age?"

And then furiously: "Drop dead, you son of a bitch!"

The boys trustingly flocked around Schlopke, and Schlopke gave them peptalks.

The General meanwhile drove to a nearby farm some three miles east of town. There he stepped into a low room and stood before the huge map on the wall. He stood before it for a long while, straddle-legged, and studied it. Then he took a red crayon and made a heavy circle around one spot.

A GENERAL AND HIS ORDER

They made him a General because he knew more than his comrades at the academy. He had a penchant for cleanliness, and no tolerance for "jerks." There are times, to be sure, when one has to put up with these characters, when they are useful. But sooner or later an opportunity presents itself to kick them in the ass.

The General thinks of Schlopke and smiles, pleased.

Aside from that, the bridge is quite forgotten: A matter well taken care of, and therefore no longer important. When the seven boys cross his mind, he has a disagreeable sensation for a matter of seconds, but then the windshield wiper inside the General's brain goes into action. Seven men. Well and good. Young chaps—still boys in fact. Most likely they're wretched on the bridge. But they have ambition, they have pride, and—they still

36

have the right kind of fear. Thank God for that. They will delay the first advance of American patrols, and that means—the General looks at his watch and figures—that means at least two hours gained.

There are still troops in the valley below, some seven thousand men. They are retreating to new positions in the eastern mountains. There is more than just one enemy in the land. A few hours might suffice. The seven thousand could be out of the valley, and on their way. If the Americans can push across the bridge, however, and break through—why then the whole valley is smashed.

The General considers further: Blow up the bridge? Now? No, that would be a mistake. If I do that, the Americans will know it before they even begin to attack. Their reconnaisance is busily at work. They won't even attempt a crossing of the bridge. They'll send up their engineers, and soon all hell and damnation will break loose. No, the Ami must be allowed to come up close to the bridge, thinking they can march across at will. Only when the first Sherman is on the bridge must the fireworks start.

They'll withdraw then, send up a few light bombers. Then it will be quiet for ten minutes, and they will advance again. The whole operation might—the General looks at his watch again—might take even three hours.

Yes—and after the first attack the bridge will have to be blown up. Just as they are about to launch the second attack. Then they'll have to send for engineers, and lose more time.

The General's hands become moist, as he stands there before the map. He paces up and down in the room.

First attack!

Resistance!

Then bombers, then second attack.

At the same moment, the bridge goes up in pieces—three hours all told.

*

The General rubs his hands together to get rid of that disagreeable moistness. He thinks once more of the seven.

But again the windshield wiper in the General's brain starts working.

7

The seven boys were inspired. Schlopke was just what they had needed. With him they'd hold the bridge. With him or without him if need be; they'd hold the bridge in any case. The General had said so.

"Do your stuff, men!" he had said.

Yes indeed, someone had faith in them. Confidence. Schlopke's peptalks had helped too.

They hung on to every word that passed Schlopke's lips. They felt they were among men now. Schlopke's instructions were sprinkled with double meanings.

"Put the machine gun over there by the stone projection!"

"There's no room for it there!"

"All right, all right! Lack of room has saved many a bitch from getting knocked up. Let's shove it over to the right a little."

"It fits there!"

They set the machine gun up at the eastern end of the bridge, behind the stone projection at the right of the bridge that formed an enclosure of sorts.

"First rate position, isn't it?" Schlopke said, and they believed it. Only Scholten expressed some doubt.

"That's no position."

Schlopke quickly cut him down to size.

"Look, sonny, don't you tell an old soldier anything about positions. Just keep your pants dry!"

Horber got busy with his tin of blood sausage, when Schlopke suddenly had an idea:

"Kids, I'm going to leave you for a while. I'll see if I can't get us some sandbags!"

And off he went. With even, unhurried steps he left the bridge, crossed the ramp and disappeared into the street leading uptown. Not a word as to when he'd be back, or what they were to do in the meantime. Nothing, nothing at all.

Horber, with his bayonet still in the tin of blood sausage, said: "Sandbags sound like a great idea. Wait till the Amis get a load of that!" He met with no response.

"Want to bet he isn't coming back?" That was Scholten.

"Of course he'll come back!" Horber was indignant. He had finally got the tin opened, but he had to tell Scholten off first: "If he doesn't come back, I'll eat a broomstick!"

Scholten: "Just make sure you don't choke on it, you stupid ass!"

SERGEANT SCHLOPKE AND THE M.P.

Schlopke pushed up the road like an Indian. Watch out, eagle-eyes, he told himself, and after every step he sized up the situation with a single glance. But he overlooked the driveway to the courtyard.

Rather, he came by it too soon. Maybe five minutes too soon. Two M.P.'s were loading the sidecar of a motorcycle. One of them stopped Schlopke:

"Your papers, Sergeant!"

Schlopke, who had gone through five years of the war without a scratch, was in no mood to take risks now, with only minutes to go before the final curtain.

"No time! Special orders from the General!" he snarled. "Secret orders, you understand? Next time! Confidentially, it's got something to do with the bridge!"

Everyone appreciates confidences. The boys on the bridge did. And now the M.P.'s. Especially since they were in a great hurry to get away themselves. The M.P. who had detained Schlopke stepped back and said: "O.K., Sergeant!"

Schlopke marched on, without any outward sign of nervousness, not too fast, not too slow. Seemingly relaxed, he was actually tense to the point of bursting. He felt the sweat break out as he walked on, and tried to reassure himself.

"Easy, Schlopke, relax, don't louse it up. If you can reach the corner safely, you've got it made. It's only another forty yards, another thirty-five yards. Jesus, what if they should come after me now?"

Thirty yards more, twenty-five yards, and suddenly he heard the sputtering rumble of the motorcycle behind him. His first impulse was to flee, to run away, to bolt. But he marched on.

The motorcycle came closer. Soon, only another second, and they've got you. Then a court-martial. The motorbike had caught up, was level with him. He did not turn to look.

Then the machine rolled past him, and one of the M.P.'s, the one in the sidecar, waved to Schlopke. The second one, who sat behind the driver, kept looking straight ahead. Then they disappeared around the next corner.

Schlopke stopped, bent over and vomited. That's from running so fast, he consoled himself. Only later did it occur to him that he hadn't been running at all.

8

Karl Horber had just about finished half of his tin of
sausage when a distant rumbling and roaring shook the
bridge.

Siegi Bernhard looked up: "I'm also beginning to
think that Schlopke isn't coming back."

The youngest of the seven had spoken in a whining
voice. Scholten, nervously: "No need to piss in your
pants right away! That's still miles away from here. And
besides, there must be more Germans before us, or the
Ami wouldn't be firing their guns."

Bernhard swallowed: "It's O.K., Ernst," and began
to cry. It seemed to have gripped Bernhard suddenly.
Forst, Mutz, Borchart, and Hager stood by, embarrassed.
Scholten was furious.

"Stop sniveling before I kick your ass in. I'll make
mincemeat out of you if you don't stop it!"

Siegi went right on sobbing, and Scholten left him
alone. He only shrugged his shoulders, and went over
to the other end of the bridge, planted himself behind

the machine gun and practiced. He put a belt of ammunition through, swung the barrel around, took the
belt out again, peered through the gunsight. Then he
came back for his sten gun and leaned it against the wall
alongside the machine gun.

"Beat it," Scholten said, "go on and beat it, you yellow
bellies. I can handle it alone if I have to."

"Not without me," Horber screamed, and joined
Scholten. Real pals those two. Inseparable. One after another they went over till Siegi Bernhard was left alone
at the eastern end of the bridge. Sobbing and sniveling,
he cowered there and waited.

The rain came down harder again. It fell in long,
even strands. The tarps and the jackets of the seven no
longer repelled the water, but soaked up the rain, and
they were drenched to the bone. Water dripped from
their steel helmets down to their shoulders and pene-
trated their clothes.

Scholten pulled the tarpaulin over his head, gave Horber the other end and they draped it around themselves.
Streams of greenish-yellow liquid gushed down to the
pavement of the bridge.

"What a God-damn mess!"

The grinding monotony of waiting was broken at
last. A civilian stepped onto the bridge and walked over
to the boys:

"Why are you still here?" He had a curiously lisping
pronunciation.

"Go on home," he said. "We don't want any trouble
here. We've lost the war."

Scholten noticed that the man had no teeth, which
was probably the reason for his lisp. Maybe he had forgotten them, or left them at home on purpose to make

44

sure he wouldn't lose them. False teeth were hard to replace at this stage of the war.

Scholten and Horber let the man rattle on. For a moment Scholten was moved to pity for the poor civilian. He felt that he was far, far superior to him. But suddenly, he didn't himself know why, he became furious.

"The bridge is being held, on orders of the General!"

Horber looked at his friend, startled by the sound of his voice—like that of a grown-up, cold and cutting. Suddenly it became clear to Horber that Scholten tried to sound like the General. That he was in effect imitating the General. It was frightening. Scholten screamed, and his high, boyish voice, which usually sounded bored and indifferent, broke.

"What are you standing around for? Scram! Get into a shelter!"

The civilian stared at them, horror in his eyes. He backed away a few feet, then started to run like a hunted animal. The boys were silent and disconcerted.

Horber laughed out loud. He held his belly, as he doubled up with laughter. "Did you see that?" he laughed on. "He jumped like a kangaroo!"

But the laughter was forced. They all knew that, and Scholten said: "Don't flip your lid!"

Bernhard had stopped weeping. Hager was the first one to notice it, and he told Borchart. Borchart told Forst and at last the news got to Scholten. He sauntered over to Bernhard and tapped him on the shoulder. "You all right again, Kid? You'll see, it won't be half so bad."

Somebody wanted to know the time. Horber and Mutz were the only ones who had watches, but they were of no use to them now; they had both forgotten to wind their watches, and of course they had stopped. There was a clock on the church tower nearby. It was ten by that clock. Ten A.M., assuming it was right.

"Chow," announced Horber, and again sat down to his tin of sausage.

It wasn't raining nearly as hard as before, and the sky in the west began to clear. They felt hungry by now, and all of them fell to their rations. They were still eating away, when airplane engines could be heard. For any experienced soldier that would have been warning enough. But they went right on poking around in their tins.

Mutz had been the first to notice the two engines. He had been sitting there on his helmet, picking the meat out of the tin with his fingers, and laboriously chewing on a piece of biscuit. The Zwieback was hard as nails.

Then he saw the planes. Two of them. Twin fuselage. Probably "Lightnings." They flew high above the bridge. He looked after them, and continued to eat. Seconds later the sound of the motors swelled to an ear-splitting din.

The planes swept across the bridge with lightning speed. There was a whistling in the air overhead that became stronger, grew to a howling, infernal roar. Some objects, looking like oblong packages, came down from above.

At a slant they drifted down, fell smack on the bridge, one, two, three. A fourth missed and went down past the railing.

The packages shot back up into the air a few feet. A burst of explosions, and then silence. The din of the motors droned off and faded away completely. Only the distant rumble continued.

Ernst Scholten lay flat on the stone slabs of the pavement.

He had hit the ground so hard that his knees pained. He thought of Schaubeck. (Lie down—up, march, maaarch! Lie down—up, march, maaarch!)

Slowly they got up to their feet again. The shock was still in their bones. As they stood staring at each other, their faces chalk-white, they suddenly noticed that Siegi Bernhard was missing.

SIEGI BERNHARD AND HIS BOOKS

"I don't know any more what to do, Herr Professor. The boy has nothing on his mind except his books!"

The short, sorely distressed woman could bear it no longer. She had to unburden herself, had to get it off her chest once and for all. It couldn't go on this way. Something had to be done about the boy. He is willing, well-behaved, does not get into scraps, but . . . he just isn't a real boy. And the little woman with work-worn hands wants him to be a real boy. Wants to see him grow up a successful man. It's for that she has toiled and slaved all these years. And now this report card! Her mind is finally made up, and she goes to see the teacher. Siegi has a "C" in German, in English, and in History. All his other grades are below the passing mark. Except for that "A" in Conduct and the "D" for Effort.

"With greater effort he could make a far better showing. The student often appears listless and absent-minded in class! Signed, Stern, official teacher." That too was in his report card.

"Tell me, Frau Bernhard, what sort of books does Siegi read?"

"He reads everything, *Herr Studienrat*. Anything and everything." And she is right.

She had tried everything. With her hard-earned money she had bought him a set for building ship models. But the fine blade of the saw snapped after only a few strokes. ("I have no knack for this sort of thing.") He had to be coaxed to go to the workbench at all. And it was only for his mother's sake that he stuck with this hobby. One day big Mutz came to the house and sat down next to Siegi at the workbench. In a few hours he completed the model on which Siegi had been working for months. When his mother came to admire the boat, Siegi silently left the cellar after throwing a sorrowful glance at Mutz.

"Knight Curtius jumped into a crevasse, because . . . ?"

Stern looks at his class: eight boys, seven girls.

"Well, Bernhard, suppose you tell us why the good knight leaped into the crevasse?"

Bernhard rises, looks at the teacher with big, dark eyes, and says softly: "He was a hero, Herr Professor!"

He remains standing without having anything more to add. But his look betrays what he would like to express: "What a man this Curtius was. Fearless and bold. Who in this class would have the courage to throw himself into a crevasse?"

"When you wake up, Bernhard, you can tell us the answer."

The teacher's voice mildly reproves him. Bernhard continues to stare up at him with wide-open eyes. If only he didn't look at one this way, Stern thinks. Suddenly Siegi feels a kick in the ankle. That hurt, damn it. But he is wide awake now and distinctly he hears the word "martyr" from the back.

"He was a martyr," Bernhard says. "A martyr, Herr Professor."

Stern has to laugh. "Sit down, Bernhard. I heard it too, Scholten. Thank you."

So much for Bernhard's performance in school. He knows what it means to jump of one's own free will into a crevasse. That is something so enormous it is hard to even talk about. Scholten can speak about it, and strangely enough the others too. And yet he alone really understands. What do any of them know about heroism? Scholten, Mutz, Forst, Borchart, what do they know? Not a damn thing. He knows. He has lived with heroes all the time, even though he is a coward himself.

Not that they ever said so to his face. Though boys their age can be mean and cruel, they had always been nice to him. Siegi knows: they are nice to me because I'm a coward. Out of pity.

He knows that in the whole wide world there is only one place where he also can be a hero. That place is his own room. All he has to do is reach for a book on the shelf, and read a few pages.

He has quite an assortment of books, all different from each other. There is, however, one element common to them all. They all describe a hero. And so Siegi is able to steer a whaler through the realms of his phantasy; all by himself, he subdues a mutinous crew on board. Magnanimously he pardons the ringleaders, although he could just as easily have them hanged. He races spirited Arabian horses through deserts, and fights victorious battles, after which he forgives his defeated opponents.

Lately he has been fighting not only for justice alone,

but also for the honor and virtue of beautiful women. Invariably these have the face of little Ingrid in the fifth grade.

One time Siegi Bernhard had the chance to be a hero. That was on Corpus Christi Day in 1943. When he came home from school the evening before, he told his mother: "There are to be Hitler Youth exercises to-morrow." His mother did not understand. Rather, did not want to understand. "We're going to the procession tomorrow, son," she said, and nothing else. Siegi is frightened: "But what do you suppose the others will say!"

"What others?" Her voice was calm, but unyielding.

"You know, the others in the class?"

"You'll have to live your own life one day, without those others of your class. Even without me, when the time comes. The important thing is what you do, not what the others do!"

The following morning Siegi Bernhard marched with the Corpus Christi procession, and was very much ashamed. The procession moved slowly up the Main Street of the town. Coming from another direction and marching towards the procession were two hundred boys in uniform shirts and short pants. They were led by a burly fellow of about eighteen. They were singing at the tops of their voices, and their song droned out the prayers that had risen in the procession. Two worlds stood facing each other. Faith and humility on the one side, arrogance and overweening pride on the other.

Would they clash?

The leader of the Hitler Youth column was only another ten yards away, and it was easy to predict the rest. The column would march through the procession, singing and shouting. The Hitler Youths would make them look ridiculous. Deliberately the leader of the column slowed down, and waited for the priest carrying the Host to come nearer.

The troopleader took a few steps forward towards the Host. An elderly man, in an old-fashioned, black cutaway coat, detached himself from the procession of believers. Calmly he walked over to the young leader and slapped his face. He slapped him twice, once on each side, with infuriating calm. Then he took his place in the procession and moved on.

The uniformed leader stopped. He had turned white, and felt his cheek. Without being told, the two hundred behind him also stopped, but went on singing:

> The rotten bones of the world
> Tremble before the great war.
> We have broken the terror—
> A mighty victory for us!
> We will march on
> Though the world be a shambles;
> For today Germany is ours
> *And tomorrow the whole world!*

But they did not march on.

The troopleader still stared after the procession with hate-filled eyes, his face now red. He turned around. "Stop singing," he screamed in a cracked voice, and walked back the way he had come. The two hundred trotted behind, disorganized, out of step, some grinning.

The procession moved forward, from altar to altar, praising the Lord without further incidents. Siegi Bernhard was no longer ashamed. He was marching beside a hero. In a way, he was a hero himself, because he marched with this procession, and not with the others. He learned that morning that courage can be found even beneath a black cutaway coat.

Scholten spent Corpus Christi Day fishing. Everybody was in town that day, and there was a good chance not to be caught. The other five went bathing. Next day they told their instructor in religion that they had to go to the Youth exercises. There wasn't very much they could do about that, could they?

Two days later, they told their staff leader that their parents had insisted on their taking part in the procession, and, therefore, they could not show up at the exercises.

They all got away with it. It wasn't the first time that they had grabbed an extra day at the beach by cheating a little. Stormtroop-Leader *Standartenführer* Forst, however, came home that night and slapped his son's face.

"Compliments of the party," he said grimly.

Siegi Bernhard had found a new hero to add to his book heroes. He could not forget the scene on Corpus Christi Day. What an enormous feat it was when a praying man subdued a fighting man! Siegi knew it was not the two slaps alone that had determined the victory, but rather the forum before which they had been administered. He dreamed that his father might have been a man like the one in the black cutaway coat. Siegi's father, alas, had been no hero. He had died in the middle of the day, at his place of work. It was after his death that Mama Bernhard moved to the little town with Siegi. He was then only three years old.

She brought him up as best she knew how. Siegi thought of his mother as an indomitable, unyielding woman. Someone to be held in awe. He was moved all the more by her complete loss of composure on the evening he had to leave for the barracks.

"Don't go, my boy," she sobbed. "Stay here with me! This madness cannot last much longer. I will hide you; please stay!" And again he had answered: "All the others are going, Mother!" But this time he was not the little boy who wanted to have his own way. This time the example of "the others" was a reproach, and she felt: He has changed, he is no longer the same. She went to his room to pack his things.

The first time he saw a hand-grenade, Siegi Bernhard clenched his teeth. Uncertain, he took it in his right hand, pulled the pin, counted much too fast, and could not wait to hurl the grenade into the air.

To be rid of it, to throw it as far away as possible. Then he crouched down and waited for the explosion. But the hand-grenade did not go off. He had not pulled the pin far enough. He succeeded at his second try, and they patted him on the shoulder: "See, Kid, nothing to it. You just gotta relax."

Yes, he stayed with it. He climbed hurdles, ran across fields, threw himself into the dirt, and almost turned into an eager beaver. But he stayed with it. He clenched his teeth, and hung on. Up to that moment on the bridge, when he realized that Sergeant Schlopke would not come back; it was then that the crude wall of camaraderie, so painstakingly built up, broke down under a torrent of tears. Far off in the distance Siegi Bernhard heard the thunder of artillery, and was frightened. Where he had usually evoked pity, he now met only scorn.

Anger and resentment welled up inside him. He stopped crying at last. He'd show them the kind of guy he was. Yes, he'd show them. But no sooner had he calmed down, when they were nice to him again.

Still, he'd show them. Hungrily he dipped into his tin of meat and ate. But when the fliers appeared overhead, he was frightened to death.

He saw the others hit the dirt, and before his eyes stood the crevasse.

Lie down, you fool! his brain hammered. Lie down!

Siegi did not listen to what his brain told him. The image of the crevasse and the brave knight stood clearly before his eyes. "He was a hero," he heard himself say, "a hero . . . a hero . . . !"

*

After the attacks by the "Lightnings," Siegi Bernhard was missing. He was actually not missing at all, only the six could not see him at first. Unlike them, Siegi was not standing. He lay flat on his face on the pavement.

Scholten walked over to him first. "Come on, Kid, those bad, bad fliers have gone again," he babbled as to a three-year-old.

Bernhard did not stir. Scholten kicked him lightly in the side: "Come on, sweetheart, can't you hear me? You can go on with chow!"

Bernhard did not move and Scholten went on clowning. Only Horber, the wild and funny Horber, noticed that there was something amiss. Rather, he sensed it.

He rushed up, took Siegi's shoulders and turned him around. There was no blood on his uniform. His eyes were wide open, staring.

"Bernhard, hey, Kid, Bernhard! Say something! Move! Please say something!"

Horber shouted, screamed at the prostrate figure and broke into loud, moaning sobs.

Bernhard just lay there. He seemed not to have been hurt at all. His mouth was half-open, slightly twisted, as though he still wanted to say something. On his right temple was a dark spot and a few splashes of blood.

They had not seen that at first. In falling, the steel helmet had slid over the spot.

9

"Damn it," Scholten said and paced up and down the bridge. Ten steps forward, ten steps back, with monotonous regularity. Then he stopped, and said once again: "Damn it."

The others squatted around silently. Hager and Forst whispered to each other. Horber still knelt beside the dead boy. His hands were folded and he looked at Siegi Bernhard's face, which was becoming more and more waxen, as though he wanted to impress its likeness in his mind forever.

He was not conscious of staring, as he knelt beside the dead body. His thoughts were far away. He did hear Mutz, the Kid's great friend and protector, weep uncontrollably. But he only just heard it. In his thoughts, Karl Horber, the cheerful Horber, stood now before God.

For the past two years he had had nothing to do with God, and now he stood before Him. Horber had a precise image of God. An old man, in a white robe, with a long silvery beard. This image corresponded to that of a painting in his grandmother's room before which he had often stood as a little boy. This image was before him now, and suddenly, after two years, he had a great deal to say to it.

Dear God, Horber was saying in his mind, dear God, why did it have to be him? Explain that; let me understand that before I go out of my mind. Why the Kid, who has no father, no brothers, no sisters, no one but a poor, old mother who is waiting for him? All alone, waiting for him. Horber pleaded, argued, was desperate. But the very next moment, his thoughts implored: Please, please, please God, if it had to be this way, since you already let it happen, be kind to him now. Take him up to you, be gracious to him, be good to him now. He had no sins. Not the least. He was so young and innocent. Look at me, I've sinned. Many, many times. But he was—was good.

The choking in his throat overpowered the wild, freckled, redhaired Horber. He sank down, bent his chest and head forward, and pressed his hands to his face. With his elbows propped up on the ground, he cowered beside his dead friend. Karl Horber wept.

On May 2nd, 1945, at 10:45 in the morning, Karl Horber wept. It was the first time since the 16th of April, 1939. His uncle had died then, and the ten-year-old boy thought that he too could not go on living.

Scholten did not weep. With clenched teeth he paced up and down the bridge and from time to time looked over to his comrades. They sat around sullen and forlorn. Horber got up, took a strip of canvas, and spread it over the body. Then he went up to Scholten: "We'll have to let his mother know, Ernst!"

"Right, Karl, but who? Who is going to tell his

mother? I'm not going to leave the bridge now, Karl. I'm going to stay on this damn bridge, and I'm going to hold it. Now especially. Can you understand, Karl? You can take him away, you can tell his mother, you can . . . you can even pray. I can't do any of these things. Not now, you understand! Now I've got to stay and fight for this bridge. That's all I can do for him. All!"

Ernst Scholten seemed transformed. They all sensed it. His eyes had a burning, fanatical, diabolic expression about them. Scholten's face was still that of a sixteen-year-old, but these eyes seemed much older. The passion and hatred of which Scholten was capable, and which from time to time had been revealed to his comrades in trivial, temperamental scenes, these burnt undisguised now in his pointed, yellowish face. The bridge had up to now been little more than an adventure for Scholten —an adventure with underlying patriotic motivations. But suddenly the General's order had come to assume a far, far different aspect. It legalized Ernst Scholten's desire to avenge a dead friend.

Within minutes, the war had ceased to be a game of Cowboys and Indians, had become a very personal affair of Ernst Scholten's. For the moment, he was completely indifferent to what the other five would do. They could leave, or they could stay. It was all the same to him. He'd lie behind the machine gun and wait. He'd wait until someone from the other side dared to step on the bridge.

His bridge, Ernst Scholten thought. He'd aim very carefully at that man, until there wasn't the slightest chance of missing. And he'd stay with him, the body, not the face. Then he'd pull the bolt of the gun back, and press the trigger. Then he'd follow every jump and every movement of the man with a swivel of the barrel and keep hammering away till the man would go down.

Yes, until then.

And then he'd say: "See, Kid, this was the first one. This one is yours." That's exactly what he'd say.

Karl Horber walked up to Scholten, looked shyly down to the ground, and told him that they had moved the body to the peaceful little square by the bridge. In the center of the square stood a monument to a dead Field Marshal, who had been born in one of the patrician houses of the little town.

"We can tell his mother when we leave here," Horber whispered, and they looked at each other.

Scholten knew that Siegi Bernhard's death had once again raised the question whether they should stay or go home. Home meant nothing to him, but he knew that for five of them it was important.

"Go on, beat it," he said again. "Don't cause your folks unnecessary grief." He had to say that. He felt it was his duty to say that. Horber didn't bother to reply, and instead got suddenly busy with his rifle. Jürgen Borchart, however, gave Scholten a piece of his mind: "Either we all go, or nobody goes. O.K.? Even if you were going, it doesn't mean that the rest of us would. Anyway, as long as you stay, we stay too. So get that into your head, for Christ's sake!"

Albert Mutz joined the group. His cheeks still showed traces of tears. "I'm staying in any case," he said obstinately.

"If I come home now," Hager grumbled, "my old folks will kill me." The Gang was laughing for the first

59

time since Bernhard's death. Restrained, to be sure, and briefly, but still laughing.

Some seventy minutes had passed since the raid. The hand on the clocktower pointed to half-past eleven.

Although they had nothing better to do, none of them wanted to think of food. Horber crossed over to the other end of the bridge, and passed the tin of blood sausage from which he had been eating so heartily before. With pretended casualness, he kicked the tin over the bridge in a wide arc as he sauntered past.

He turned around abruptly, and was angry when he saw that the others had watched him.

The boys were suddenly startled to hear artillery quite close. Only about four miles away. Certainly not more, certainly not more.

"From the way it looks," Horber said, "the fun ought to start in another half-hour, at the most."

"If not sooner," Mutz ventured despairingly. But Scholten reminded them again that there must be more Germans ahead of them; the Ami isn't shooting for the fun of it.

"High time we got busy!" Scholten snarled. "Who takes the second machine gun?"

Horber screamed: "Me," before Mutz had a chance to say anything. Mutz was hurt. He was, without a doubt, the better shot. But Scholten, who had taken over undisputed command, was satisfied with Horber.

"Well, then it's all settled," he said, pleased. "Mutz is coming with me to take charge of the ammunition, to feed the belt and to steady the tripod, if it wobbles."

He turned to Hager: "You can do the same for Horber! Forst'll take three bazookas, and station himself behind the rampart. You, Jürgen, take Horber's automatic rifle and get up into that old chestnut tree!"

They were delighted with that last suggestion. Great!
A terrific idea! It was clever of Scholten to think of it!

The chestnut tree stood on the western bank of the
river, some twenty yards away from the approach to the
bridge. "Take the carbine along too. You never know
when these automatics go on the blink," Scholten ad-
vised. "Also, take as many clips with you as you can carry
and hide up there. Take the whole pile of them. You
know, Jürgen, you can't climb down to get more during
the battle. Better get set up there for a long time. Get
the idea?"

Jürgen confirmed that he did indeed get the idea. He
was grateful to be told all that, because on his own he
would hardly have thought so far ahead.

Jürgen sheepishly grinned at Scholten and spread a
piece of canvas on the ground. After that he got a box
of cartridges and started to fill clips. Hager joined him,
then Forst. Finally the whole Gang sat there filling clips,
as many as they had.

They all looked once again at their cartridge pouches
and counted to see if they had sixty shots apiece. Hager
was shy five, and took them from the canvas. Scholten
checked the two magazines of his sten gun and found
them both loaded.

"Let's get started," Scholten said, and went to get
three bazookas. He carried them over to the rampart at
the western end of the bridge, behind the wall projection. He motioned to Forst to come over. "Walter,"
he said, "I know you are a cool bastard. We all know it.
I have an idea how you can get them—look down
there!"

Forst, who had colored at Scholten's compliment as

though it had come from a General, leaned over the railing. Between the river and the walled-in bank was a strip of gravel, some ten feet wide, which the water had deposited in the course of years. The first arch of the bridge spanned the strip as well.

"If you stand there under the arch and look out to the road, you have an unobstructed field of fire extending some forty yards in front of you. That should do it. They'll never find out who is knocking their tanks out of commission. And they must come up this way. There is no other road to the bridge."

Forst was all aglow. This was just how he had imagined it would be. He took two bazookas and carried them down to his hide-out under the arch. He returned for two more. He kept this up until there were only two left above. When he wanted to take these too, they protested. Horber squawked: "You can leave us some too, even if your father is a big shot in the party!" Forst did not take it amiss. He had heard it too often. And besides, it was true.

He knelt under the bridge with the bazookas and proceeded to wire them. When Scholten took Forst's carbine down and saw that, he stopped short: "What the hell are you doing? You can't wire them all in advance and pile them up like that. One swoop and you'll be blown to smithereens!"

"In that case you'd better scram, Ernst, or you'll come with me," Forst said, and smiled in a friendly way, showing his white teeth.

He went on fixing the bazookas. "I know," Forst grinned, "I always lacked the proper respect!" He looked into Scholten's face.

"Good luck, Walter!" Scholten said simply, and put

out his hand. But Forst ignored it, and went on making fun of him.

"Scholten," he said, in perfect imitation of *Studienrat* Stern, "recite for us . . . Hölderlin's poem: *Death for the Fatherland* . . . 'The battle . . .' Come on, Scholten . . . continue, you old sleepyhead!"

Scholten, who was usually cynical and sarcastic himself, felt chilled; he was anxious to get away from this spot under the arch, to join the others above. But the laughter seemed to pursue him as he ran up. Funny, he thought later, I'm all right now, but while I was with Forst I felt strange. I felt very strange. I almost think it was fear. And I already forgot little Bernhard, Scholten thought. Yet, I must not forget him. As long as I don't forget him, I am not afraid. Yes, that's it. I'm not afraid then.

He thought of Bernhard, and worked himself up into a rage again. A cold, malicious rage. And he felt: Unless they come soon, I'll no longer be able to feel this rage.

Borchart had meanwhile stowed all his equipment in a canvas. He hung his rifle over his shoulder, then the carbine. He asked Hager to help him with the canvas, and they walked up to the tree.

"We'll need a rope," Borchart announced, "or we'll have to take everything up separately."

"Where are we going to get one?" They noticed the lifeboat below the bridge. It was moored to the bank with a heavy rope.

Horber ran down and tried to cut the rope with the bayonet. But he only succeeded in shredding small fibers. He finally put the rope on the beam of the raft and hit at it with the bayonet as with a machete. He

63

returned with the rope, and they helped Borchart establish himself in the tree. All except Forst, who was sitting by his bazookas below, singing of the red sun in Mexico.

"Get behind the trunk," Scholten suggested. "Preferably on a heavy branch. Hang the carbine within reach and keep the ammunition next to you. Also you'll have to steady the automatic to hit anything."

Borchart said: "Thank you, thank you, thank you," grinned, and climbed like a monkey up the heavy trunk.

"All you need is a red ass and you'd look like a mandrill," Horber joked. Then he thought of Bernhard, and felt ashamed.

Borchart shouted down at last that he was as comfortable above as in an easy chair, and he let the rope down. Then he pulled the rest of the stuff up, and busied himself stowing it away.

As the four stood below and looked up, the man who had been on the bridge earlier that morning walked by again. This time there was a little woman with him, and she trudged by his side with short, quick steps.

"Tell me," he asked, "are you really going to put on a show here?"

He seemed rather subdued this time. "We're going over to a friend's house. They have a better cellar. There isn't a soul left on our side," he said. "Haven't seen a human being all day."

"We are not putting on a show," Scholten said. "We have an order to hold this bridge, that is all. Do you understand that?"

The man walked on, the woman tripping along at his side. "We are holding the bridge," he said, "with a handful of children!"

"That guy is bad luck," Horber whispered. "I already thought so this morning!"

"Just an old windbag," Scholten growled. "Nothing but an old windbag."

Scholten was getting into a nasty mood again.

He got hold of Mutz and pressed two machine-gun cases into his hands. Then he slung his sten gun over his shoulder and picked up the machine gun. They crossed over from the right to the left pavement, and took up a position behind the stone projection which extended about two feet into the pavement.

Scholten set the machine gun down and lay behind it, while Mutz climbed down to the riverbank to fetch some of the big stones that were left behind when the bridge was built. He dragged four of them up to the bridge.

He stacked the stones up along the wall projection in such a way that the barrel of the gun peered out as from an embrasure. Scholten made sure that he had enough room to swivel the barrel about freely. He had to adjust the stones once or twice before he was satisfied that all was in order.

He went over to Karl Horber and Klaus Hager and pointed to his machine gun: "Look at that and do the same on your side."

Horber and Hager went over to inspect the set-up. They liked it, and went to the riverbank for stones. They dragged up twelve stones, some so big they both had to carry them, and built a substantial wall alongside the bridge projection on the right.

Scholten looked on. Horber said, grinning: "I am doing this for my health, Ernst, you understand!"

The thunder of artillery that had startled them earlier had ceased. But they had been too busy to notice it before.

Suddenly each of them felt the deadly stillness. Not a sound was heard outside the murmuring of the river; down below the bridge Walter Forst sang: "Who rests, rusts . . ." Borchart up in his tree seemed to doze. The other four stood around.

"If that guy would only stop singing," Hager moaned; he was green in the face. "I swear he's driving me nuts."

Forst went on singing:

> Down in the valley there is grass, there is grass,
> Down in the valley there's hay, yes hay.
> Every time I see my lass, yes, see my lass,
> I feel so very gay.
> Lassie keep smilin'
> Till we meet once more,
> We're off to England and the U.S.A.,
> To quickly end the war!

"Shut up or I'll kill you," Hager screamed down; but Forst just laughed, and sang on:

> We were anchored before Madagascar
> And had the pest on board.
> The water in the kettles was putrid,
> And daily someone went o'erboard.
> He longs for his sweetheart, who at parting
> Had kissed him, oh so tenderly,
> And looks out across the ocean
> Where his far-off home must be.

Forst sang, and Hager did not kill him. But he said: "For heaven's sake, think of the Kid."

After that there was quiet. Absolute, oppressive quiet.

66

Hager was tempted to go down to Forst. To tell him: "Go on, sing. I didn't mean it that way."

But Forst remained grimly silent. From time to time they heard the clanking of the bazookas as he handled them. Aside from that, the only noise came from the river itself.

Horber looked at the tower clock. It was a quarter past two. It could not take much longer. Over in the west all was quiet too; no artillery fire, no noise of combat. Scholten mumbled, "There must be more Germans ahead of us, or they would not have fired the cannons."

He was lost in thought, when he suddenly heard a motor. All listened as the sound came nearer, growing louder.

"A tank," Scholten shouted. As it rounded the corner and came up the road, it presented an excellent target for the machine guns, for Forst's grenades and Borchart's automatic rifle. But it was not a tank. It was only a battered German truck to which infantry men were hanging on, clustered like bees on a beehive.

The truck clambered up the bridge, driving at a snail's pace, and stopped. The driver screamed over to the boys: "Are you blowing the thing up?" Scholten yelled back: "No, we are holding it!"

"I'll be damned," the driver said. "Let's get the hell out of here, before someone gets the bright idea of using us as replacements." He stepped on the gas pedal, in a hurry to be gone. Scholten ran alongside the old truck.

"How close are the Yanks?" he shouted. "Are there more Germans in front of us?"

"Not now, there aren't!" the men shouted back from the truck. "We're the last. They'd have gotten us, too, if it hadn't been for this old jalopy. Some more cut across the river, two miles up. The Ami is taking his time."

The soldiers screamed some more, but Scholten couldn't understand a word. He ran as fast as he could but couldn't keep up, and soon quit.

Slowly, he walked back to the bridge, his chest heaving. From time to time he threw his arms up to take a deep breath. He had learnt that in gym classes. His chest felt freer again. He threw himself behind the machine gun. "I think it's getting serious now, Mutz. They were the last. But they say the Ami is taking his time."

Mutz had nothing to say to that, and asked: "Do you happen to have a cigarette? I have to have a smoke or I'll fall asleep."

Nobody had cigarettes left. They had all smoked their last. "I know who has some," Horber said, speaking slowly, stressing every syllable.

Then he motioned with his shoulder to the monument, to where Siegi Bernhard lay under a strip of canvas. Tears welled up in his eyes. Mutz sat on the floor, and started to sob, and Scholten said: "Damn it all."

Forst, who had joined them, sauntered over to the monument. The others did not watch him. He returned with half a pack of cigarettes and held it under their noses. Mutz said: "I don't feel like smoking any more." But Forst replied calmly: "Go on and take one. They're no use to him!"

They all smoked.

They sat on their steel helmets. Their thoughts circled around, and always returned to the same point, to Siegi Bernhard, the Kid, sissy Bernhard.

Horber said softly: "All I want to know is why him. There are seven of us, why him?"

"He was crying before it happened," Mutz recalled. "He must have had a premonition." Hager shook his head: "He was crying because he was scared. Because he was scared it got him."

After a brief interval, Scholten said pensively: "It was him, because it was his fate." But Borchart quickly rejoined: "No, it was him because he was the weakest."

Forst shrugged it all off: "All nonsense. It was him because he didn't lie down. If he had hit the dirt the way he should have, he'd never have gotten that splinter in his temple. He was just a child. All of this was not for him."

Horber still stared into space. "Maybe the Kid was just dreaming when it happened, thinking of all the big deeds he would some day accomplish in his life?" Albert Mutz best understood what Horber was driving at. "I really loved that guy; we were together a lot," he said with a sob. Scholten knit his brow. "Don't talk rubbish, Mutz. We all liked him, each in his own way. But no one loved him."

"I did so," Mutz persisted stubbornly.

"What you call love," Forst said harshly, "is only pity. And you can stop feeling that for him now. He's had it. Anyway, you are not really sorry for him—you are sorry for yourself now."

Horber came to Mutz's defense. "Mutz is right, I too loved him. He . . ."

"Cut it," Forst interrupted savagely. "He is dead. Too bad. But we can't change it. Sure, we are sorry and sad about it. But why speak of love. Anyway, you can only love dames!"

Borchart looked at him. "You mean women, Forst," he asked, "is that what you mean?"

Before Forst could answer, Mutz said sullenly, "I don't even know what you're talking about, what it's like to love a dame."

There was a halt in the conversation. With one exception, no one knew much about that. And even this one thought of something else. They were all thinking of something else, and Hager spelled it out: "I don't think dying is so very dreadful." Forst pulled a face. "Dying maybe not, but being dead. Just try to imagine! Everything you have, and do, what you are, all that is suddenly no more; is over and done with. Oh you lonesome valley—how dreadful that is!"

Hager had paid no attention. He was still musing: "It is only dreadful when you know about it ahead of time. But you never do. And you go on hoping you'll be spared. I certainly hope so now."

Scholten said: "All a question of fate!" Mutz: "You call it fate. When the shells start bursting, I'll say the Lord's Prayer." Forst, mocking: "You'll hardly have time for that!" Mutz, calmly: "There's always time for that."

They fell silent. They felt great fear now, and if one had suggested it, they might all have left. Even Scholten; even Forst. But they were too ashamed, and stayed on. As if he owed the others an explanation, Mutz finally said: "I'm staying because of him there!" He pointed to the monument. They knew just how he felt.

"A damn good reason," Scholten said. "In a way it makes it easier for us."

"What do you suppose Stern would say to all this?" Mutz wondered suddenly. Their thoughts turned to their teacher.

He was one of those rare human beings who made friends everywhere. A severe illness had left him crippled when he was still a little boy. The pity he encountered when he returned to school, after a long convalescence, struck him like a blow; pity had engulfed him on all sides, and he was carried along by it.

Fellow students treated him with kindness. Teachers helped him. "How is it going?" the instructor would ask, while the class was brooding over a math problem. Then the mathematics instructor would lean over Stern's shoulder and help him. The class did not mind it. They silently accepted that this one needed to be helped.

But the pity gnawed at Stern's heart, and while his body grew more deformed and hunchbacked, his mind became clearer and freer. He came to realize at last that a healthy and alert mind can exist even in a crippled frame. He studied harder, crammed for exams. Though he dutifully turned the light off when his mother came to bid him good night, he turned it on again ten minutes later, and spent half the night poring over his books.

When the First World War cast a shadow across the land, Stern graduated from high school at the top of his class. Along with his classmates, he volunteered for service, but he was not along when they marched triumphantly to the railway station, amidst cheers and the sound of martial music. He stood behind the windows of his room, and through the blinds stared down at the street below. The words "unfit for military service" gnawed at his heart as the pity had formerly done. He was studying in the almost empty lecture halls of the university when the first letters began to arrive from the front. By the time the first casualty lists were published in newspapers, including the names of friends and school comrades, he was working as a part-time tutor. As he stumbled through the streets at night, hunchbacked and deformed, he felt the shame of staying at home while others were bleeding in the war. He volunteered again, but they couldn't use him. "Be glad we don't want you," they told him. "Thousands would be only too glad to get out of it, and you complain."

Shortly after the war, he got his degree. Then came Gisela. Quite unexpectedly she had walked into his life; he had met her in a nightclub, where he was carousing with some young colleagues. He walked her home that night, and knew by the time he left her at her doorstep that she corresponded to an ideal he had been seeking in vain. They spent beautiful months together. Then summer came, and Gisela began to turn down his dates because she wanted to go bathing, or rowing.

Once he went along. He put on a pair of swimming trunks and waited for her on the beach. At long last she came running up in her blue bathing suit, an image of bodily perfection, and he stared at her. He sensed pity in everything she said that afternoon. He struggled against it, but he didn't want to lose her. Two days later he accepted a friend's invitation, and took Gisela along.

They got off to a good start. They had coffee on the terrace, and later one of his friends asked Gisela to a game of tennis. Hunchback Stern sat on the terrace and watched them exchange volleys. Gisela easily dominated the field, as she nimbly dashed about on the tennis court, joyously happy and carefree. He stood up and left. He never saw Gisela again. The following day he left the city to take on the post of substitute teacher in one of the provinces.

He was a good teacher, an expert in the subjects he taught, but he was a poor educator. Students feared him. He was just, but hard. This was to change one day. A little fellow, new in his class, came up to Stern, and looking at him with big, trusting eyes, asked him whether he would consent to take on the crafts group of the class. Some of them wanted to build little boats, but they had no one to assist them, to supervise. Suddenly it became clear to Stern that this little boy had come to him because he needed help and confidence, not out of pity, and that he had accepted his deformity as a matter of course.

Gradually Stern got to know his students better, learned to love them with that innate capacity of his to like all people. With untiring effort he prevailed on the school administration to put one of the rooms in the attic at his disposal. With his own money Stern then laid the basis for the crafts department which was later to become the pride of the school. They spent many afternoons there at the workbenches, hammering, sawing, filing and polishing the naked hulls of their boats.

The big day came. They took the boats to a swimming pool for a race. When Stern saw the boys kneel at the edge of the pool to set their models into the water, he knew that these boys were his life's work—work he could do, even as a cripple. When they later set up a pingpong table in a second room, and Stern found that he was able after a short time to beat almost all comers, he thought of Gisela.

"What a fool I was," he told himself.

That winter he took his class to a ski lodge for two weeks. At times he was troubled by his infirmity, but the respect and confidence of his students invariably helped him over it again.

Next he was assigned a small class. Seven boys and eight girls. He had never before established such close contact with a class; he looked forward to seeing their young faces every morning. He worked hard to encourage the best in each of his students, and to help them over their shortcomings. He knew his students well, and got to understand them even better when he came to know their parents.

That evening, as the Americans drew nearer to the town and the din of battle echoed from the bridge, Stern stood in church and prayed: "Heavenly Father, spare my boys."

10

The boys sat silently, each pursuing his own thoughts. It rained only lightly now, but their tired bodies felt chilled.

Forst passed the pack of cigarettes around again. There were only four left. They divided three between them, and Forst put the pack with the last cigarette back into his pocket. They sucked away at their half-cigarettes. A raindrop extinguished Scholten's, he tore the damp end off and relit the butt. The paper had absorbed too much moisture, however, and came apart.

"Shit," he said, and flung the cigarette into the puddle which had formed on the bridge between pavement and road.

They crouched on their helmets as though they had completely forgotten why they were there and what still lay before them. It wasn't long before it was brought back to them.

A hum and a rumble rose up in the distance and crept incessantly closer. They jumped up, electrified, listened, stared west, and then looked at each other. Six chalk-white faces, and big, unnaturally big, burning eyes. They put their helmets on. Not a word was spoken.

Borchart raced to the chestnut tree. After a few quick movements, he grabbed the first branch, and like a monkey pulled himself up and disappeared in the foliage behind the trunk. Walter Forst walked leisurely down the ramp to his bazookas, still puffing away on his cigarette. Scholten sat down behind the machine gun on the left, then lay down and peered over the gunsight through the hole between the projection and the pile of stones. Albert Mutz opened the two machine-gun cases and got everything ready. He let the belts glide through his hands again. Horber threw himself behind the machine gun on the right, and motioned to Hager to open the cases and insert the belt. They lay in ambush, their nerves taut to bursting.

Horber felt the tension mount and take hold of him. He was tempted to pull the trigger lightly, just once, to let the gun rattle a little, only to break this unbearable tension.

But he did nothing; he lay there and waited like the rest. The din of the motors had become louder meanwhile. It can't be much longer. Soon they'll be here. What will it be like? Albert Mutz asked himself; what is actually going to happen? I wonder how long it takes to die, and if one knows it when it happens? Or if only the others will notice it? ("Ah, they got Mutz too!")

I wish they'd come, Scholten thought. I wish they'd come. I can take this for another minute or two at best, but not longer. Certainly not longer. I'll count up to a hundred and twenty. By then it will just have to start.

And Scholten started to count. One, two, three, four, five, six, seven, eight . . . thirty-three, thirty-four, thirty-five. But he gave it up.

Borchart, in the tree, thought of nothing. He crouched behind the trunk and aimed the automatic rifle out to the road the Ami had to come up. He felt like a charge of dynamite. All he had to do was curve the right index finger ever so lightly, and the charge stowed up inside him would explode. He was toying with the trigger, pulling it back lightly, and letting it snap forward to its resting point.

Hager nudged Horber. "I think it's starting now," he said. The four on the bridge and Borchart up in the tree were suddenly startled to hear someone whistle.

It was Walter Forst. They could hear it distinctly. For although the whistling sounded rather thin, it yet stood outside of the approaching din of motors.

Walter Forst whistled the old song:

> Today Germany belongs to us
> and tomorrow the whole world.

There was something insidious, diabolical about this whistling. He had better stop it, Scholten thought, or I'll go out of my mind.

Suddenly he remembered something. Something terribly important. He had to tell the others before it was too late. He got up and ran over to Horber, crouching down all the time. Then he dashed over to the chestnut tree and shouted up. Last he ran down to Forst below the arch.

The whistling stopped. Slowly, Scholten came back and lay behind the machine gun again. He had told the others not to shoot before he had given the signal.

"Maybe the Amis will fall for it," he reasoned. "Maybe they'll think there is no danger here for them. Maybe they'll just come marching up here, unsuspecting. There isn't a thing to be seen on the bridge. They'll hardly count on meeting up with any resistance here."

Suddenly, they heard the humming of airplane motors, over and above the rumble of the approaching tanks.

They needed no one to give the order now. They jumped up from behind the machine guns and raced down both sides of the bridge to Walter Forst, for cover. "Fine shelter you picked," Forst said, grinning, and pointed to his bazookas.

They could not see the planes which circled the bridge two, three times. They only heard the motors and waited for the shrieking sound to pierce the air. Ready to throw themselves into the dirt, to bore their fingers into their ears, open their mouths wide and wait. But they didn't have to.

The sound of the motors diminished, droned off in the distance and died down completely at last. Christ, I bet they're off now to make a report: Not a soul left on the bridge. It's all in order. And their General will say: All right then, let's push on! And he'll march his army forward.

The six on the bridge had gotten used to the rumble of the tanks. It had become louder so gradually that in the end they could no longer distinguish an increase in the noise. The first Sherman was rounding the corner, just as Hager was saying to Horber: "Christ, I have to take a leak now."

"You can't take a leak now," Horber hissed. "You should have thought of it sooner." At the same moment

Scholten yelled: "They're coming! They're coming!"

Horber and Hager both turned with a start and looked straight ahead at the road. All of them now saw the gray-green colossus move up the road with a grinding clatter. Slowly and heavily the monster rolled nearer. And then they saw the people, moving along the housefronts on the right and on the left. Soldiers in olive-green windbreakers, with rifles in their hands, funny-looking straps around their legs, and round helmets on top of the olive-green jackets.

Slowly and cautiously they moved along the line of houses on either side of the road, stepped into a driveway every now and then, came out again. Once they raised their rifles with a sudden threatening motion, pointed them at the windows of an upper story, waited a few seconds, and moved on.

The tank was about two hundred yards away from the bridge. Some eight or ten yards behind the tank were the men in windbreakers. Alert and watchful, they moved on towards the bridge. Behind them, the boys saw a second tank rounding the corner into the road, and then a third. Soldiers armed with rifles crouched in a thick pack on these two tanks, peered into every direction, and seemed ready to jump off any moment to take cover behind the nearest building.

The first tank was only a hundred yards or so away from the bridge now. The infantrymen were level with the tank. Borchart sat up in his tree, and looked back and forth from the approaching Americans to Scholten. Forst, a bazooka crammed under his arm, stared at the road from behind the bridge ramp. He strained to hear a signal from above. Horber looked over to Scholten and motioned to him desperately to get started.

79

Hager thought: Damn it, I've got to take that leak now. I've got to . . . and suddenly felt helpless to stop the water running from him. Scholten and Mutz, behind the left machine gun, kept their eyes on the tank grinding forward, and on the watchful figures in olive-green uniforms along the rows of houses on either side. With clenched teeth they stared ahead. The straps of their helmets were pulled tight, and gave their boyish faces a hard, manly look. Ernst Scholten surprised himself. I wonder how much longer I can take this, he thought.

ERNST SCHOLTEN AND JOHANN SEBASTIAN BACH

Albert Mutz's mother was a remarkable woman. The man she had married twenty years before, and to whom she bore two sons, turned out to be a failure in life. He was a failure in his profession, and a failure as husband and father. Another woman in her place might have put up with it for two or three years at most; then she would have taken the two boys, and run away. Back home to her parents, or elsewhere. If she had looked anything like Frau Mutz, it would have been elsewhere. But she stayed on with her two children.

Most men would have given a lot to have a woman of Frau Mutz's charm and beauty around them, would only too gladly have cared for her, spoiled her. She looked young enough to be sometimes taken for Albert's sister. And Albert was the younger of her two sons.

He loved his mother. He was proud of her when they walked side by side to church on Sunday mornings. It made him happy to look at her. Especially on those evenings when she sat at the piano, and worked her fingers along the keys to play the immortal music of Bach, Chopin, and Beethoven. Albert sat at his mother's feet, closed his eyes, and let the music carry him far, far away.

One evening he brought a skinny, scrawny kid along to the house. He didn't look like much of anything— this boy with his pale, sickly face, and the wild, unkempt, jet-black hair.

"This is Ernst Scholten," he said to his mother. "He likes music."

The mother did not take to her son's school comrade. A little black devil, she thought secretly. But the next time Scholten came to the house, he brought his flute along and joined in her playing. He was only fourteen at the time, but he played with such consummate skill and so much passion that the woman at the piano was often tempted to rest her hands on the keys and watch him.

"Your mother is a remarkable woman," Scholten would say after such evenings, and his usually gruff voice became soft. Albert Mutz felt a little jealous.

What about this Scholten? How was one to understand him? How was one to get at the bottom of that enigma? He was fresh in school. Enormously fresh. Yet he opposed the entire class when they wanted to put a thumbtack on the chair of the religion teacher. He asked the most pointed questions on religion in his class, and when all religious instruction was halted in school, he went over to the rectory twice a week, along with some of the other boys. Yet the records showed he was an agnostic.

Scholten lived on a farm outside the little town. His parents had sent him there when the air raids in his native western city had become ever more menacing. He had no objection to leaving. He had never seen much of his parents, even at home. His father was always on the go, always attending meetings, conferences, conventions. His mother spent her time visiting friends, going to charity functions, and sometimes receiving friends at home. "Go to bed, Ernst," she would tell him then.

The mornings after, the glasses could be seen all over the parlor, some still half-filled with whiskey. And the room was permeated with the odor of his mother's sweet French perfume. How he hated this perfume! There wasn't a soul he could tell that to. There was no one he could talk to about anything. On a shelf in his room were books by Spinoza, Schopenhauer, Rilke, and even a single volume of Nietzsche, sandwiched in between the second and third volumes of Karl May's *Winnetou*. He was an avid reader, but he was not able to digest everything he read; as a result it was a strange, confused, wavering view of life that began to take shape in his mind.

It was all different on the farm. He rose early enough to watch the milkmaids milk the cows in the stable. With playful ease he learned to perform most of the chores around the place. He went to school on his bike, and spent many afternoon hours rambling through the neighboring wide woods. Two small-caliber rifles hung in his closet, and he sometimes took one of them along on his jaunts. Occasionally he shot a hare, a wild duck, and once even a roebuck which he brought back with him. He was well aware that hunting was illegal, but he had no scruples about that. He knew: I mustn't be caught at it, or they'll kick me out of school, and there'll be a terrific row. That alone, not his troubled conscience, bid him be careful.

He loved fishing. For hours he sat on the bank of the

river, or waded barefoot in one of the innumerable brooks, casting out his line. Often he left both fishing rod and rifle home, and roamed aimlessly through the woods. Many an evening he took his flute outdoors, sat on some treetrunk, improvising soft, dreamy melodies.

The nights in his small room were long. Especially the summer nights, when the humidity pressed in through the open windows and dark storm clouds gathered in the west. For hours he'd lie sleepless on the coarse linen, bathed in perspiration. When he heard the young maid bustling about in the adjacent room, he toyed with the idea of going over. To see what it was like. But he would not have been Ernst Scholten had he gone.

Once, on an unbearably hot summer afternoon, he ran down to the river nearby, threw off his tattered pants, pulled the checkered shirt over his head, and jumped in. He lay on the flagstones of the embankment afterwards, and looked up into the cloudless blue sky, till a sudden noise startled him. He walked towards it, some thirty yards downstream, forced his way through the willow bushes, and saw two people lying in the sand, struggling. He wanted to run up, but stopped short. The two weren't struggling after all. Blushing, he walked away from the spot. He dressed hastily. So that's it, he thought, so that's what it is like. He slept no better afterwards, but he was no longer tempted to go into the next room.

Every now and then he met with his classmates. Invariably he came up with some idea. Twice, they swiped all the eggs from a chicken farm and feasted on mountains of scrambled eggs. They made eggnog with what was left over, and, drinking it, even Mutz and little

Siegi Bernhard lost whatever scruples they still had. Such was the nature of the orgies they were able to have from time to time. A few cigarettes pinched from father's desk, a jar of preserves from mother's cellar, and sometimes even a bottle of wine.

Once they went out to explore the deserted mine in the hills outside the town. Armed with flashlights they entered the tunnel. Borchart, Hager, and Horber soon refused to go any deeper, and left together with the Kid. Undaunted, Mutz, Forst, and Scholten pressed on till they reached the end of the tunnel. They encountered nothing in particular, and turned around to go back. Every now and then a lump of soil came loose overhead, sending a shiver down their spines, but not one of them would have admitted it.

Suddenly they heard a muffled thud. They raced down the tunnel and found themselves blocked in by a wall of soil, rubble, and stones. They all realized the situation they were in.

"Let's go," Scholten said, pale as death. "We've got to work our way out!" He put his flashlight out, and the three of them climbed up the mound of rubble and began to dig furiously with their bare hands.

"If this muck gives any more, we're done for," Scholten whispered. "But we have to risk it."

They didn't know how long they had sweated at it, when Forst cleared a small opening through which he wriggled like a snake. It sounded as though it came from far off when he called to them: "I'm through." Mutz and Horber followed through the same hole, and slid headlong down the mound to the other side. Silently, they walked to the exit.

When they saw a glimmer of daylight, they started to

run. Only when they were outside did the impact of what they'd just been through sink in fully. "That was close," Scholten said, and spit on the ground.

They laughed, embarrassed. They saw their four comrades playing Cowboys and Indians, and went up to join them. Halfway, Scholten turned to the others. "Let's keep that to ourselves," he said.

The government organized the free time of the youth. They had meetings every Wednesday afternoon in the arena, or in the clubhouse. Scholten was an outsider here as well. He never went to meetings, didn't own a uniform, and his name was probably not even carried on the organization list. This didn't prevent him from telling Stern some Thursday mornings: "I beg to be excused, Herr Professor, I couldn't study the poem yesterday. There was a Hitler Youth meeting."

Scholten did not say: "I was at the meeting." He merely said, "There was a meeting." To him that made all the difference in the world. The one was a trick, the other a brazen lie. And Scholten did not lie. If the teacher had asked him how long the meeting lasted, he would have readily admitted: "I wasn't even there." And would have taken his demerit with dignity. Nor would it have been the first.

The day Scholten got his draft notice, he packed his belongings. He took his rucksack in the left hand, his flute in the right, and went to Mutz's house. Patiently he waited for Albert to finish packing. Then he asked Frau Mutz: "Please, play once more!"

Silently she sat at the piano and played.

Ernst Scholten meanwhile walked up quietly to the big closet, opened it carefully, and put his flute inside.

"Well, so long, Mother!" Albert said, and took his

rucksack. His mother stepped over to the little font next to the door, dipped her finger in, and made the sign of the cross on her son's forehead. She put her arms on his shoulders and kissed him.

Scholten stood aside, his eyes hard and searching.

"God be with you, son," she said to Albert, and her eyes met Scholten's dark eyes staring out of his white face. She walked up to the gloomy boy, put her arms around him. "Take care of my boy, and of yourself!" she said.

"Well, so long, Mother," Albert said once again. And Scholten, stiffly: "Farewell, dear lady!"

Only after they had left, did it strike her that he had said "farewell." And later in the evening, when she put the sheet music in the closet, she saw the flute.

*

Ernst Scholten loved life. He lay behind the machine gun now to carry out some General's order. But was it still for the sake of that order that he stayed on? Was it not something entirely different that had taken hold of him since? Something inexplicable that compelled him to stay on?

Ernst Scholten hugged the butt of the machine gun. His finger was on the trigger. The tank was only some ten yards away. The soldiers fifteen, possibly twenty.

"Now," Scholten said and bent his finger. Then he felt the thrusts of the gun against his shoulder.

11

The six boys had had fourteen days of basic military training, but a few drills and a hasty explanation of weapons was the extent of it. If they succeeded at all in taking the Americans by surprise, it was only because they had chosen and maintained their positions in total disregard of all military considerations; because they defended the bridge against all the accepted rules of strategy. This ambush was strictly Indian stuff—something boy scouts might count on, but certainly never trained troops.

Ernst Scholten felt the painful thrusts of the machine gun against his shoulder. He had sighted along the barrel, and aimed at a single figure in olive green. He did not swerve about wildly, but kept the gun on this one man alone. "Hold steady, Mutz! Damn it, hold steady!" Scholten screamed. Mutz lay on his back feeding the belt through with one hand and holding the machine gun stand with the other. Scholten kept his finger on the trigger. He saw the man keel forward slowly, very slowly, and went on shooting till the soldier hit the ground full length.

Karl Horber was shooting away with his machine gun like a maniac. He screamed at the top of his voice, his face distorted, and shot at the soldiers along the house fronts. Then all hell broke loose.

The tank spit fire like a monstrous dragon, veering from one side of the street to the other. The air vibrated with the sound of exploding shells. The soldiers, except for the few that lay unmoving in the road, disappeared. The four boys on the bridge were now at the receiving end of the gunfire. Bullets clattered against the wall, ricocheted off the stones.

Scholten shot blindly into space, swiveling the barrel about like Horber now. They had gone through one belt, and Mutz, with nervous, quick hands, was getting the second one ready. Scholten put it in place, but it jammed. He had to open the receptacle again, and to adjust the belt. Then, grim-faced, he pulled the trigger again.

Only one so far, he thought, as he suddenly saw Siegi Bernhard, the Kid, before his eyes. He spotted the Americans again. They had withdrawn to the houses, and lay behind the windows of the upper stories shooting angrily. The tank on the bridge ramp still ground back and forth, and spit fire like some primeval monster.

Jürgen Borchart crouched behind the treetrunk. He had early exchanged the automatic rifle for the more familiar carbine. "Can't hit anything, you piece of shit," he said as he reached for the carbine. Well out of sight, he aimed at the windows, one after another. The Americans had no idea where the shots were coming from, and were seemingly surprised. Every time a soldier came to the window to look out and shoot at the machine-gun nests, he made a perfect target for Borchart. Two soldiers drew back in horror after he pressed the trigger, and a third one stayed on the window sill with his arms hanging down.

Walter Forst had waited under the bridge till the shooting started. He now lay some distance away from his safe hide-out, and observed the tank. It veered right and left, firing from all guns, and once came directly at him. Forst was sure he had been spotted, but the tank turned halfway around and swiveled the turret in the opposite direction. Seeing this repeated a few times, Walter became cool and calculating.

The men in the tank hadn't seen anything so far, he concluded, or they wouldn't scatter their fire so aimlessly. He got a bazooka ready and lurked. I must aim it so that it will hit between the turret and the hull, he thought. If I can ram it down there, it'll finish them off.

The tank came up close to his side once more. Why don't they just drive on across the bridge and finish us off from behind? Walter asked himself. But almost immediately he knew the answer to that. They must think we're a belated demolition squad, waiting to see them go up in smoke.

"Next time he comes up to my side," Walter said, "I'll let him have it. You can bet your sweet life on that," he threatened the tank.

The tank lumbered over to his side. "If you make a turn now, you're done for," Walter whispered, and his eyes sparkled. He lay there waiting tensely. The tank made half a turn again. Forst took careful aim, and fired.

A flare of fire shot out of the tube under his arm. Seconds passed, minutes, hours—it was the fraction of a second only—when the cover of the tank shot open, and heavy smoke rose from its hull.

The tank swerved around, grinding, rattling and clamoring like some drunken colossus.

Then it stopped.

"I got him," Forst yelled, "I got him. Hey, kids, I knocked a tank off. Hooray!"

Walter seemed to have gone berserk. Shots rang out from all the windows nearby, while he stood upright next to the bridge, doing an Indian war-dance. The others watched with grim joy as the tank went up in smoke.

A cool customer, a real cool customer, Scholten laughed, and kept shooting at the windows.

"I'll let him have one in his ass." Borchart gnashed his teeth. "So help me. If he doesn't scram, I'll burn his ass."

But Walter had already disappeared. Like an eel he dived into his shelter. The two other tanks now came up the road. Without infantry. The soldiers had all taken cover, the devil only knew where. Probably in the houses.

The Shermans came within twenty yards of the bridge ramp and fired. Their turrets turned and let loose a barrage of fire, alternately aiming at the right and left machine-gun nest. Scholten lay behind his gun and raced the third belt through. He even shot at the tank. Lunacy, he thought, sheer lunacy. Shooting at a tank with a machine gun!

Still, he went on shooting. Horber, too, kept up the barrage. Borchart was the first to spot the soldiers up on the rooftops. They lay in ambush behind the chimneys, and having a free and unobstructed range, fired down at the machine guns. Forst crouched by his bazookas. He was cursing because the tanks came no closer. "Move up a bit, damn it. Come on closer, so I can knock you off."

Forst, that madman, ran up with a bazooka towards the nearest corner, and fired it at one of the two tanks. He missed, and like a hare ran back under the bridge. Just look at that idiot, Scholten thought.

Borchart had been closely watching the man in the garret across the way. He was only waiting for him to stick his rifle out and also his head. If he wanted to hit Forst, the man had to stick both out of the window. He did not get Forst. He let the rifle fall and disappeared behind the hole.

"Damn it, damn it," Forst moaned. "What a beastly trick. I just barely missed!" He lay under the arch of the bridge weeping with rage and frustration.

The Americans seemed to have improved their positions, or else had gotten reinforcements. Although one couldn't see a single one of them, their fire had become heavier. The tanks gave them the most trouble. "If only I could get close to them," Forst was raging under the bridge.

Suddenly he had an idea. He'd take two or three bazookas and crawl down the riverbank. Then he'd force his way into one of the houses from the rear entrance, look for a window facing front, and knock out the tanks from close up. He was angry at himself for not having thought of it sooner.

Walter Forst took two bazookas from the pile, and started out. Pressed flat against the stony ground, he inched forward, creeping downstream away from the bridge. If anyone sees me, he thought, I'll get a bullet in my back. There isn't a damn thing I can do about it now.

He had no idea how long it had taken him to reach

the first house. He stood up, and ran towards it, crouching. The house, like the others on the street, had a door facing the river; it was there the people sat to rest when the day's work was done.

Forst pressed the handle of the wooden door, and stepped into a dark hallway.

A man stood before him. "Get out of here. Get out this minute. I don't want any trouble, you hear! Beat it!"

"Shut up," Forst said rudely, and shoved the man aside. If he should slap me, Forst thought, I'd probably lose my wits. And he'd be within his right to do it.

But the man did nothing of the sort. Frightened, he danced behind Forst, and pleaded with him. "Please leave. The Amis are already in the house. Fight outside. Spare my little house!"

Forst, suddenly alert: "Where are the Amis?"

"Up on the roof. Look, they'll get you anyway. All of you. Why don't you beat it while there's still time?"

Forst had heard enough. He stalked along the corridor with his two bazookas, and stepped through the last door. It was the toilet.

How ingenious, Forst thought, as he stepped on the bowl to look down. He was nearly scared out of his wits. The one tank was maybe six yards away from him.

Almost close enough to touch. He put a bazooka under his arm, and pressed down. The toilet filled with smoke. I'd better get out of here, he cautioned himself. They can see the fumes outside on the street.

He threw the door open, raced out into the hall, and found himself face to face with a strapping American.

For the fraction of a second, they stared into each

92

other's eyes. Forst with the second bazooka in his hands, the American with a rifle.

Forst put the bazooka down against the wall. The American followed his every move. Forst threw his hands up, held them high above his helmet, and slowly walked back. The American followed him, just as slowly, keeping his rifle aimed at him.

Forst felt the doorhandle in the small of his back. Now or never, he thought, and hoped the owner hadn't locked the door.

He leaped suddenly aside, flung the door open, and with another jump was out on the street. He heard the wood of the door splitting two, three times.

The American fired.

Forst ran on. By the time the American opened the door to look down along the river, Forst was already lying under the arch.

He recovered his breath, and after a while felt tempted to look up to the bridge ramp. He edged forward, and when he saw the second tank standing in smoke, he was filled with pride. The third tank had vanished.

Probably gone for reinforcements, he thought.

Then he remembered with horror the confrontation in the hallway. He cowered behind the arch of the bridge. I have my fill of heroic deeds for quite a while, he thought.

Explosions rocked the air around him. Walter Forst became suddenly aware of how unspeakably tired he felt. If only this mess here were over, he wished. Still later he thought: Oddly enough, I'm not even afraid. Does that mean I'm a hero? Or does it simply mean that I'm just stupid?

Then he reminded himself again that he had knocked out two tanks, and was pleased. But the feeling of joy was short-lived. He had up to now only been thinking of the gray-green, smoking steel boxes. Suddenly it struck him: Christ, there are people inside these tanks. Human beings, the same as I.

He shuddered at the thought of the smoking hulls. I hope they send no more, he said to himself. I don't think I could do it again. Damn it all! He trembled. I wonder how many people there are inside a tank? He was startled out of his reverie. One of the two machine guns on the bridge had ceased firing.

Scholten and the rest on the bridge had not followed Walter Forst's maneuver. They had been kept too busy. Shells whistled sharply above their heads. They hit the projections and the stones behind which they lay. Stone fragments whizzed through the air, or whistled past their heads. Suddenly they noticed that the second tank was ablaze. Scholten and Mutz looked at each other. Horber and Hager stared bewildered into each other's faces. No one knew how it had happened. It couldn't have been the machine gun, could it? Whatever it was, the tank was out of commission. The third Sherman drove off.

Threatening, it swiveled the turret around, emitted a ray of fire every now and then, and finally disappeared in the direction from which it had come.

The soldiers had, however, established a firm foothold. The four on the bridge bore the brunt of it. They had the impression that the Americans had even managed to edge forward, and had meanwhile improved their initial positions.

Scholten saw one of the olive-green figures in the driveway of a house, and pressed the trigger of the machine gun. The machine gun sputtered once, and immediately fell silent. Scholten pulled the chamber open.

The black tin of a cartridge had gotten stuck and jammed. He couldn't pull it out. He tore the machine gun from the embrasure between the wall and the pile of stones, picked up the sten gun which leaned alongside him, and put the butt against his shoulder. Then he pressed the trigger.

He fired single shots.

I mustn't waste any, he thought. Who knows what still lies ahead of us?

Jürgen Borchart felt certain that his tree was shell-proof. Not a single shot had strayed in his direction. He fired away as on the rifle range. With calm deliberation. He too had seen the American in the driveway.

I wonder what he wants, Jürgen Borchart thought, and adjusted his sight. The American lifted his rifle, and aimed at the gray spot in the chestnut tree. I think he has it in for me, Borchart thought. I must beat him to it!

JÜRGEN BORCHART AND THE IMPORTANCE OF
PHYSICAL TRAINING

Height: 5′ 9″; weight: 136 lbs.; color of eyes: blue; color of hair: blond. Fine posture. Disciplined. The sort of youth parents can be proud of.

"So you want to become an officer, Jürgen?"

"Yes, Papa!"

"Have you given it sufficient consideration, my boy?"

"Of course, Papa!"

"It's a hard profession, Jürgen. The keyword is obedience, and it's not always easy to obey. You may have to do certain things of which you don't personally approve. And they treat you pretty rough, my boy."

"I understand that, Papa. One just has to get ahead far enough!"

"What do you mean by that?"

"I mean one has to advance to a position where one gives the orders, and then one can do everything right."

"But only a few go that far. The rest have to obey, all their lives. Sleep on it, son. You can apply tomorrow just as well. It doesn't have to be today."

"It does so have to be today, Papa!"

This conversation between Colonel Klaus Borchart and his only son Jürgen took place in December, 1944, in the study of the Borchart apartment. That very day Jürgen sent off his application, with all the required data. In the evening, he and his mother saw his father off at the station. His leave had expired. He was returning to the front.

Colonel Klaus Borchart kissed his wife good-bye.

With a firm handshake he then bid his son farewell. "Don't disgrace me, son!"

The train started to move. Colonel Borchart came to the window of his compartment. They waved until they lost sight of one another.

A week later Jürgen received a notice to appear for an examination in the capital city of the province. He went, and was examined physically, was weighed, measured, and tested for athletic prowess. He gave quick and precise answers to the many questions they put to him, and left a splendid impression behind. Two weeks later, he received preliminary notification that he had been accepted as an active candidate for Officer's Training School. He was as happy with the printed little slip of white paper as if it were already his Lieutenant's commission.

The same mail brought a letter with a black border. Colonel Borchart had fallen on the field of honor on the very same day on which his son had passed his tests for the military academy.

"Withdraw your application," his mother demanded.

Jürgen said: "No."

"If you have a shred of honor left, withdraw the application!"

"You aren't logical, Mama. I can't withdraw my application. Precisely because I have a sense of honor. What do you suppose father would say if I withdrew my application now?"

His mother kept quiet after that. Not just for a day or two—she persisted in a bitter, inconsolable silence, and confined herself to the few words necessary in their daily life.

Sometimes he attempted to break through the barrier between them. "Try just for once to understand me, Mother. I can't do it. I'd have to hide for shame!"

His mother flared up. "Nobody ever tried to understand me! Your father didn't, and you do even less!"

He gave up.

Try as he would he couldn't comprehend his mother's attitude. He had never failed. Not in school, not in athletics. He was always among the best in his class. Why then did she want to force him into an act of which he would be ashamed?

He didn't understand that his mother was driven by the fear of losing him as well. Of receiving another black-bordered letter in the mail, and a few days later the wallet with the last mementos of her only son.

Jürgen Borchart was the best athlete in his class. He

97

finished the 100-meter dash in less than twelve seconds. He leaped way beyond the six-yard mark in the broad jump. In the high jump he cleared five feet easily. He could hurl a shot across the width of the arena, was the fastest swimmer, and lost only once in boxing. To Forst of all people.

He had not lost because Forst was stronger or faster. Uncompromising, Forst had led off immediately with a straight hook at Borchart's nose, while it took Jürgen two rounds before he decided to hit at the face that danced and swam before his eyes.

He too succeeded in landing a couple of punches, with the result, however, that Forst hit even harder and proceeded to belabor his nose even more systematically, as he danced around Jürgen like a little devil. Borchart was glad at the time that the instructor halted the bout. But he could never get over Forst's victory, though the decision had been eminently fair.

Jürgen Borchart was no longer used to losing an athletic contest to anyone in class. Physical training and discipline played an important role in his daily routine. It started every morning with a cold shower and setting-up exercises, push-ups and deep knee-bends. The physical training was resumed in daily gym classes, and found its culmination in the afternoon, when he raced alone across the track. He ended each day with a second cold shower, and at least ten push-ups near the open window.

Whenever Jürgen detected a weakening of his will power, he mercilessly castigated himself. With these tried and true means he believed he had full control over his body. He was convinced of that. Until that day when he forgot his sneakers in the shower room of the gymnasium, and ran back for them after class. He left the door of the gymnasium open, ran into the shower room, and froze on the spot. He reddened, stammered: "I beg your pardon," and dashed out.

Siegrun Bauer kept right on twisting and turning under the shower, and laughed after Borchart as he was running away. Miss Bauer was the girls' gym teacher. She was twenty-seven. She did not believe in closed doors.

Whenever Jürgen saw her on the street, he crossed over to the other side. But he couldn't avoid her in his room at night. He saw her body before his eyes as soon as he turned the light out. On such evenings he tried twenty push-ups, and he tried even thirty. Once he got up to sixty and collapsed. Still, he could not control his body this time.

The class liked Borchart. But he wasn't taken too seriously. He had too often set his will against the class, only to be won over in the end. Each time his prestige suffered a little.

When Jürgen got the notice to appear in the barracks, he was disappointed—he wanted to become an officer, not part of the big herd. But he shied away from doing something about it because of his classmates. And now he sat up in the chestnut tree near the bridge. He had sighted the American who in turn held his rifle aimed at him.

*

I must be quicker than he, Jürgen thought. I must hit him, or I'm sunk up here. That guy has spotted me, for sure!

Jürgen Borchart was not quicker. Ernst Scholten heard the rustling and swishing in the branches of the chestnut tree. Then a hollow thud.

The clips from the canvas came rushing down like

hailstones and fell on the body below the old chestnut tree.

Farewell, Jürgen, Ernst Scholten thought.

He had been gripped by anger when little Siegi Bernhard fell, but all he felt now was a deep pain. He toyed with the idea of putting down his rifle and running away. He looked over to Horber, who lay behind his machine gun and fired away. He seemed not to have noticed anything. I only wonder who he is shooting at, Scholten thought wearily.

Albert Mutz had grabbed his carbine and fired shot after shot, in short intervals. The man who had killed Borchart still stood in the driveway. Scholten felt hatred well up inside himself again. It almost pleased him to note how rage could cover the pain. He switched his sten gun over to automatic action, pressed the butt against his shoulder, sighted the man in the driveway, and pulled the trigger.

The barrel of the rifle bucked, pulled upward. With all his strength he tried to keep it horizontal. But the man disappeared as soon as the first shells struck the wall.

I'll have to let the others know Borchart is dead, Scholten thought.

12

How long had the exchange of fire been going on? The boys on the bridge would not have believed it if told that since the appearance of the first tank scarcely thirty minutes had passed. They only knew this—it must not go on much longer.

They were tired, apathetic, close to quitting. Only the instinct for self-preservation prevented their getting up now and running away. Even Scholten no longer thought of the General's eyes and of his order. He wanted to get away as much as the others, wanted to crawl home, into his bed. Wanted to awaken the following morning, get into his tattered civilian pants, slip on his checkered shirt, and wander. Wander far away from the noise, the explosions and racket. He wanted quiet, nothing but quiet. Above all, he wanted to leave the bridge alive; he didn't want to stay on and die.

Two have already been killed, he thought. And for the first time something akin to anger came over him, anger at those who had left them here alone.

He was startled by what happened next. One of the Americans, a short, stocky fellow, dashed out of a driveway like a runner leaving his starting position on a cinder track. With short, quick strides he raced to the chestnut tree next to the bridge. He stood behind the mighty trunk before Scholten could turn his sten gun around and fire.

What does he want? He's probably going to finish us off with a hand-grenade, Scholten thought. Still, along with fear, he felt a liking for the man. A first-rate runner, he thought. A fine athlete.

The barrel of a rifle came out from behind the tree, then an olive-green shoulder, an arm, and at last even a head. The face beneath the steel helmet was white.

I can hit him easily now, Scholten thought. He is careless.

But he kept his finger on the trigger without pressing it. The American leaned against the tree. He also held his fire. He wants something, Scholten sensed. The soldier began to shout at them:

"Stick 'em up, boys. Stick 'em up, we don't fight kids!" And then in broken German: *"Krrig vorrrbei, mak snell, sonst kaputt!"*

I'll give him a chance, Scholten thought. I can't help it, but there's something about him that I like! And with deliberate slowness he pulled the rifle up to his shoulder.

The American promptly disappeared behind the tree-trunk. Only then did Scholten press the trigger and pump a round of shots into the tree. Almost immediately after it, the American popped up from behind the tree.

"Give up, you son of a bitch, or I'll blow your brains out," he yelled over. Scholten again pumped a round of shots into the tree. Long splinters came flying off the bark.

Then the American raced back the same way he had come. Scholten and Mutz looked at each other. "A crazy bastard," Scholten said, and: "I just can't do it, though. I haven't got the heart to do it."

The soldier had covered about half the distance back. Scholten and Mutz were staring silently after him when the machine gun on the right suddenly sputtered briefly. One, two quick bursts of fire.

The American was only about seven yards from the driveway when he reeled halfway around, raised his left hand to the sky as though taking an oath, and let the rifle fall out of his right hand.

He hit the ground hard, rolled over, and writhing with pain, beat wildly about with his legs. He screamed. Only once before had Scholten heard anybody scream like that. That was the Kid, little Siegi Bernhard, who now lay still beside the monument. It was the time he had been hit in the stomach in a soccer game.

The American writhed on the ground, and screamed. Everything else seemed to fall silent, every other noise died down beside that frightful howling. Albert Mutz pressed his face to the ground, let go of his carbine, and put his hands to his ears. He couldn't bear to listen to this. I didn't want to do it, Scholten prayed. I didn't want to do it, so this stupid ass goes ahead and shoots.

He was furious. He turned around to Horber. "Look at it, you shithead, just look at it. Finish the job. Go on finish him off, you shithead, you started this!"

But the American was suddenly still. Very still.

And Karl Horber didn't reply. He lay speechless behind the machine gun, and when Klaus Hager shook his shoulders, he rolled half over on his back.

KARL HORBER AND THE GUILTY CONSCIENCE

He himself did not know why, but as far back as he could remember, he always had a guilty conscience. He was always making some mistake, doing something wrong, saying something insulting, or forgetting something important. He didn't want it that way at all. Quite the contrary—he was anxious to do things right. He wanted to be a good boy, a good student, a "useful member of society," as his father, the honorable master barber Fritz Horber, called it.

Karl Horber made his first mistake at his birth—he caused his mother's death. He was certainly not to be held responsible for that, yet it affected all his later life. Master Horber could never look at his son without being reminded of his mother. Then he'd sigh and return to the shop, to shave and cut the hair of his customers, and to talk with them. There was no joy in the house since the mother had passed away. Fritz Horber felt he had been singled out by fate; that whatever happened, happened to him alone.

Karl Horber saw to it that something happened all the time. Trivialities mostly, but now and then more serious things. One day a policeman came to the shop, saluted stiffly, and said to the elder Horber: "Sorry to be the bearer of sad news. Your son Karl was run down by a car. He's in the hospital. Seems hopeless, I'm afraid."

The policeman cleared his throat self-consciously and left the store while Fritz Horber stared uncomprehendingly at the razor in his hand.

Well, hopeless though it seemed, little Karl Horber was home again in three months' time. And in another two weeks was as fresh, as clumsy, as forward as ever. "It'll take more than a car to keep my boy down," his father said, not without a trace of pride, when his customers talked to him about it. Maybe it was the freckles, the red hair, or the protruding ears that turned Horber into the quick, witty little boy he was. He had discovered early that he could not charm people even with the prettiest curtsy or an obliging readiness to be of service. He wasn't an amiable child, and didn't try to appear like one.

From the first grade on they kidded him about his looks with such regularity that he soon got used to it. The kidding became less frequent. Of course there were still times when they went at him almost on cue. Then Horber did what came easiest by nature. He laughed the loudest at the jokes aimed at him. They liked that about him. Sure, he was a blabbermouth, but they got used to that too. He was well liked.

Yet hardly a day passed on which Horber didn't get his face slapped, or receive a demerit. He simply had no luck. When three of them broke a windowpane, the policeman didn't go to Mutz or Horber, he showed up in the barbershop, and, with a look of genuine compassion for the sorely tried father, related the latest misdemeanor.

He reported these incidents in a voice that implied: "You and I both would have been spared a great deal of sorrow if it had indeed been hopeless the time he was run over." The policeman looked on broken windows as a serious offense which he dutifully noted in his weekly reports.

Only it wasn't just broken windows. When a barn burned down one night and witnesses declared that it had been the work of youngsters, the policeman went first to his old friend Fritz Horber. Karl, right off the bat, got the indispensable slap in the face, even though he steadfastly denied any part in it. It took some time before he admitted that he had been to a movie that night—it was a film "for adults only." Master Horber felt relieved and at the same time reassured. His son was not guilty of the arson, but he had deserved the slap just the same.

Horber was a fairly good student. He would have been a better student had he worked harder. He never picked up a book unless he was in danger of getting a poor grade. "Eminently gifted," Stern said of him, "but extremely lazy."

Once at a chemistry examination he answered all the questions in short order, and then gave his paper to Walter Forst, who had been sending him desperate signals for help. When Forst had finished copying he returned the paper to Horber.

A week later they got their grades. Horber received an "F." "Copied word for word from Forst," said his paper.

It didn't help any when Forst went to the teacher and told him what had happened. "Nice of you to be so honest," the teacher said to him. "I have no choice but to give you an 'F' as well now." It made Walter Forst seriously question the wisdom of helping a friend, if you only harmed yourself in doing so.

Such questions did not occur to Horber; he was basically a coward. It was that which may have accounted for his willingness to go along with any nonsense. Karl Horber had, largely because of his big mouth, acquired a reputation for being a daredevil. He anxiously guarded that reputation.

The favorite pastime of the class was the "I dare you" game. The rules were simple. As soon as anyone talked big, he was encouraged by the rest: "I dare you." Unless he was a coward, he dared.

Scholten, Mutz, Forst, Hager and the rest found themselves in a situation where they had to play the game maybe once a month. Horber almost daily.

Once Stern assigned a great deal of homework over the weekend. Horber arrogantly bragged: "You know what I'm going to do? Not a damn thing. That's what I'll do. Monday I'll just walk into the class and I'll say: 'Excuse me, Herr Professor, but there were too many assignments!' "

But he didn't have the slightest intention of going to school without his homework, he was only showing off as usual, making himself appear to be a tough guy. The class knew that too. No sooner had Horber finished than they shouted at him from all sides: "You wouldn't dare, Horber!"

Horber realized immediately that he had been shooting his mouth off again. He couldn't possibly admit that, and appear a fool before the class. He'd have to go through with it.

When Stern asked for the assignments on Monday, the lean, redhaired Horber stood up, and with faked calmness crowed: "Excuse me, Herr Professor, I don't have my homework. It was . . ."

"All right," Stern interrupted before he could go on. "We'll talk about it after class."

But Horber couldn't let well enough alone, and started again. "Herr Professor, it was . . ."

"I said we'll discuss it after class!"

The honor of the show-off was at stake, however, and Horber, without stopping, said:

"It was too much, that is why I didn't do my homework, Herr Professor."

Well, he had said it. Now let anyone tell him that he didn't dare. He dared just about anything. But Stern was not to be taken in that easily.

"Come, Horber," he said, "it seems to me you're rather nervous about something. Go on out for a while, and get some fresh air. Come back when you feel better!" There were repressed giggles in the class, and Horber felt that Stern had gotten the better of him.

After class he went to apologize. "Sorry, Herr Professor. I did not mean it badly. I didn't want to appear like a coward before the class!"

"Horber, suppose I tell the class what you just said? What do you say?"

Horber colored. "I'd rather you didn't, Herr Professor," he said meekly.

"See here, Horber—I call this a serious shortcoming: to annoy your teacher in order to play the big shot before the class."

Horber apologized again. He said that he hadn't thought it through sufficiently. That he had just got himself into a spot, and then couldn't back out. Stern looked at him silently for a while. Then he said: "Horber, you know I can put up with a great deal. I was also a rascal once. But I wish you wouldn't forget what happened today. In the future try to think of what you're saying!"

Horber was glad to be let off that easy. He promised to be more careful. At the time he made the promise, he was firmly convinced he'd keep it. But only two hours later, during the last recess, he said to his friends: "It's a crying shame to be locked up in class on a day like this. One ought to cut the last hour and go bathing!"

Laughter, and again shouts. "You wouldn't dare, Horber. You'll chicken out this time!"

Without giving it another thought, Horber went to pack his schoolbag, and left.

Calmly, he stalked out of the schoolyard, and went to the swimming pool. It was only after he got there that it occurred to him he had no swimming trunks along. Disgruntled, he trudged home. In the afternoon he was the subject of a teachers' conference. In spite of Stern's intervention he was put on notice again, for the third time. Once again Master Horber had to "go to Canossa," and beg the principal for a reprieve.

The one and only time Horber went fishing with Scholten they were caught. That is, Horber was caught —Scholten, as usual, was able to disappear before the owners of the pond caught up with him.

The policeman called on Master Horber in the shop, and again Karl had his ears boxed. But he went on insisting that he had been alone, and that the owners were mistaken when they claimed there had been two. Because of Master Horber's good name, no charges were pressed. This affair too was straightened out without further consequences.

There was only one catch. Fritz Horber demanded an accounting from his son of every minute spent outside. Visits to friends were forbidden, let his friends come to his house instead.

Up in his garret they could carry on as much as they

pleased. Forst and Mutz especially were frequent visitors. The barber did not object to their studying at times late into the night.

Their studies ranged pretty far afield. They'd play "chaining," for instance. One of the boys would be tied with ropes. The other two timed him to see how long he took to break loose. Or they performed chemical experiments. Always with the same objective in view: the manufacture of gunpowder. Once Mutz brought some indefinable compound too close to the flame, and the whole thing blew up with an enormous racket.

Old man Horber stormed up the stairs. "What happened? For heaven's sake, what happened?"

When he saw the singed eyelids and eyebrows of the boys, their faces soot black, but otherwise unharmed, he raged. "Who the devil teaches you this nonsense?"

"Our chemistry instructor," Karl Horber replied softly, and without flinching took the powerful slap his father administered.

After the incident with the gunpowder, his friends stayed away from his house for some time. And Horber, for his part, showed a surprising reserve.

"Our little Horber hasn't got himself a sweetheart now, has he?" Forst once teased him. Horber promptly blushed. But Forst apparently hadn't noticed it, and he didn't pursue his insinuation further.

Something had indeed entered Horber's life, something that aroused a strange curiosity in him. His father had hired a new assistant, a girl of about twenty-two. She had long, pitch-black hair, a dark face that gave her appearance a gypsy-like quality, and green, slanted eyes. Over her white coat she wore a narrow, black belt, pulled so tightly that Horber more than once asked himself how she could possibly bear it.

Her coming to work and live in the house changed everything. Father Horber gave her the second room in the attic, the one right next to Karl's. He believed, and with good reason, that he knew his son in this one re spect at least. Outwardly, there were hardly any changes noticeable in Karl Horber's daily life, unless it was that he showed up more frequently than usual in the shop to ask irrelevant questions.

Or that he spent evenings home much more often, and went up to his room surprisingly early. In what relation he stood to Barbara—that was her name—he himself didn't know. Unconsciously, he sought to be near her, and he stayed home when he knew she was in the house. But when she addressed him he blushed, gave meaningless, inane answers, and left the room. Sometimes he believed he was in love with Barbara; then again he felt repelled by her, by the way she walked and talked, the way she sauntered through the shop when strangers walked in whom she'd measure with an appraising look, at once interested and cool. Attraction and a desire to run away were the conflicting feelings she evoked every time he came near her. And on top of that, there was his curiosity.

One day he cut a small wooden peg, then he went to the cellar for the heavy, wooden hammer. He put the peg against one of the bigger knots in the wooden partition that separated his room from hers. With a few thrusts he drove the knot through. Carefully, he hammered a little nail into the knot, so that he was able to put it back in place or pull it out any time he wanted. He smoothed the knot down with sandpaper, and oiled it.

That evening, he went to bed earlier than usual.

When he heard her come up the stairs, he turned the light out, got quietly out of bed, and tiptoed over to the wall. With one pull he had the knot out of the wall. He pressed his left eye against the opening. His heart was beating so loud, he was afraid it could be heard next door.

She entered her room. It isn't nice what I'm doing here, Karl Horber thought. It isn't nice, damn it. But she doesn't know it. No one knows it.

The most contradictory feelings surged in his breast. Once he came close to crawling back to bed, but his curiosity won out in the end.

He had to wait a long time. Barbara lay down on the bed, put her head on the white pillow, took a cigarette and matches from the night table without looking. She lay there staring at the ceiling, and inhaling the smoke in slow, deep draughts. The cigarette seemed to last forever. Karl Horber felt the cold from the floor creep up his naked legs, and a second time was close to slipping back to bed.

But just then Barbara got up, threw the white coat over the chair next to her bed, and undressed. He lost sight of her for a while, but heard her pouring water into the washbasin. Heard her washing, drying herself, and brushing her teeth.

Nothing at all unusual about any of the sounds, Horber found. Really, hardly exciting. He saw her step up to her bed, watched her put on her nightgown, throw the blankets back, and turn the light out. That too wasn't exciting.

Not the least bit.

But in spite of that, Karl Horber stood again at the partition the following evening, put his eye to the opening, and heard his heart beating. It was the same on the third day and on the fourth day. After a week's time, that quarter of an hour at the wooden partition became a part of his daily routine. It is my secret, Horber thought. A secret he was not going to share with anyone. He wouldn't even speak of it in confession.

They had all gone swimming to a pool, and were lying in the bright sun. A lazy afternoon. Suddenly Forst had a notion. "Let's go in the water, dive under the wood-partition and have a look at the women's section."

They were all for it. Mutz, Forst, and Scholten. Only Horber declined.

"Christ, what you can see there is just the thing to spoil your appetite for good," he said precociously. Lazily, he turned over on his back, and blinked in the sunlight.

"You're full of hot air," Forst snapped back. "You're only against it because you're afraid to swim over."

That was true. Horber was a poor swimmer and afraid to go in deep water.

They laughed.

Whereupon Horber forgot, as usual, his solemn promise to Stern never again to show off.

"What you can see there, kids, I can see any day of the week," he said indolently. "And close up, too. Just like the movies!"

His three friends perked up their ears. What was Horber keeping from them? Forbidden books? Or pictures? These things circulated among them, every now and then. Not too often, but still every now and then. Forst knew exactly how to handle Horber to get something out of him.

"You're just a show-off, Horber!"

"What am I?" Horber crowed. "You take that back, or I'll punch you in the nose!"

But Forst didn't give in. "Proof, Horber," he said provocatively, "we want to see what you've got to offer. Anyone can shoot his mouth off!"

Heatedly, and without giving it another thought, Horber: "All right. At eight-thirty tonight, you come up to my room. For a game of skat, agreed?"

They met in his room that evening. Hager had a deck of cards. A night lamp stood on the little, round table in the center of the room. Between the table and the wall, there was a fire screen. "Hey, let's have some more light in here," Mutz demanded as soon as they walked in.

"Can't have more light than that," Horber whispered secretively, "or the movie doesn't work. It must be completely dark on this side of the room."

He had a guilty conscience, and was scared. For one thing he was afraid that there was still too much light, and that some of it might show through the knothole into the other room. Then he explained: "Listen, kids, we're playing skat now. Later on we'll get up, one after another, and you'll do just what I do. If you've got anything to say, talk about the card game—nothing else. Is that clear?"

They sat down at the table and started to play. Since there were four of them, one was always out of the game. Later on they heard steps coming up the stairway, and Horber said: "I'm playing solo now!"

He put his cards down, stepped over to the wall and took a peek through the hole. Then he stepped back and motioned to Hager to take his place. Hager stood there gaping until Horber finally pulled him away by the sleeve. "Give somebody else a chance to get into the game, Hager."

Forst took one look through the hole, then glanced

back to the table and blinked knowingly. After a while he turned around, and took his place at the table again.

"I grant you, Horber, pretty tempting!" He grinned cynically.

Mutz was the last. He stood at the wall and stared.

Damn it, she is attractive, he thought. A really pretty little thing.

And then he felt sorry for her. He turned around. "Horber, this is mean of you," he said. "It's a downright mean trick. I wouldn't have expected it from you."

Horber anxiously put his finger to his lips, and winked at Mutz. "Have no fear, Horber," Mutz said. "I'm not going to spoil your game. Only don't expect me to play along!"

He took his coat from Horber's bed and left the room, banging the door shut behind him.

"Think nothing of it, Horber," Forst consoled him. "He'll never be a decent card player. Hager, you deal," he said, turning to him.

But Hager did not want to play any more either. He felt that Mutz had acted hastily. Almost like a schoolmaster. Yet somehow Mutz was right, Hager knew.

He felt ashamed before the beautiful, black-haired girl in the next room, even though she didn't know him. The evening ended disagreeably. Forst also left.

Horber, at last alone in his room, was miserable and depressed. His big mouth had again gotten him into a horrible situation. Now they all knew his secret, and worse, Mutz, whose friendship he valued highly, was mad at him. But when they met in school the following morning, Mutz seemed as friendly as ever. Horber decided to bring the conversation around to the previous evening.

"Don't be sore, Albert," he said. "You know I meant no harm."

"I know," Mutz replied in a friendly tone. "If I didn't know that, I'd have punched you in the nose last night. I'm not angry because of that knot hole. It's that you bragged about it, that's what's so awful. Do you understand? That we all know it now, and that she doesn't. And that you'll hang again at your peephole tonight, and tomorrow night. That she has to put up with this disgusting business night after night, thinking she is alone and safe in the privacy of her four walls. Can't you understand that, you greedy little snotnose?"

Mutz said all this with restrained, friendly voice, but Horber could sense that behind it there was still a residue of anger. He tried again to win his friend around.

"I'll seal it up, Mutz. I promise. Today!"

"I take your word for it, Horber," Mutz said, and his voice was no longer restrained, but open and clear as usual.

As he walked home, Horber was still determined to seal the hole up. But when he passed through the shop to get into the house, he saw Barbara. She was leaning over the table, reading a newspaper. The peephole stayed open. Karl was still the first one to retire to his room, night after night.

He stayed away from Mutz, and avoided all contact with the big, blond boy whose eyes could be so penetrating at times. Otherwise, Horber still kept shooting his mouth off as usual. On only one subject did he hold back. He no longer talked lightly and frivolously about women. If he happened to be with a group when an off-color joke was being told, he had the feeling that Mutz was standing behind him and looking right through him with his clear, steady gaze.

Horber would then turn around suddenly to reassure himself that Mutz wasn't actually there.

Three of them had never participated in these conversations. Mutz, Scholten, and little Siegi Bernhard. Borchart and Hager listened, without ever contributing much to the discussion. Horber and Forst had usually been the spokesmen. That had changed now. Horber had become a "still water," his friends joked.

One day Horber knew for certain that he was in love with Barbara. He knew not only how she looked; he knew other things about her as well. Most important of all, that she was alone. And the loud-mouthed Horber desperately tried to think of ways to change his relationship to the strange, dark girl.

He kept up his secret spying on her, but more and more often he felt ashamed of it afterwards. More and more frequently he swore to himself that he'd seal the peephole in the thin wall between their rooms for good. But at night he lay on his bed again, and waited for the sound of her footsteps.

One evening he was again standing at the partition and watching Barbara prepare for bed. Then he heard other, heavier steps come up the stairs, and heard a soft tapping on the door of the next room. He saw Barbara turn, saw the door open, saw a man enter and turn the light off. He had only caught a glimpse of the face, but had recognized his father.

That night, Karl Horber didn't close an eye. He wanted to weep, and was surprised that he could not do so. Next morning he sealed the hole. When he came home from school at noon, he found the draft notice waiting for him.

He thought it was best that way. He couldn't look into his father's eyes when he took his leave of him. And when his father told him to say good-bye to Barbara, he merely shook his head.

"Don't you worry, Karl," his father said, "we'll mind the store here!"

"Sure you will," Karl said. He took his rucksack and the schoolbag full of food Barbara had hastily prepared for him, and left.

His friends made it easy for him. That very evening Karl Horber was laughing again, was as spirited as ever, and thought of home only at times. He had quickly resigned himself to carrying on in his accustomed role of braggart and joker. To playing the clown for his friends' enjoyment.

His humor left him only on the bridge, when he saw Siegi Bernhard dead.

*

He clung to his machine gun and fired away, fast and furiously. When he saw the one American run from the chestnut tree to the house, he automatically swung the barrel around and fired until the man collapsed. The unusual relationship that Scholten and Mutz had established with the American had completely escaped him. Who knows where his mind was while he lay behind the gun? He thought of his father, of little Siegi Bernhard, of Barbara—and fired away. He did not hear Scholten screaming over to him. He could no longer hear it.

As he was firing the second shot at the running American, something hit his forehead, was going to split his head in half. His eyes, as though set in burning, red circles, seemed to float away. Darkness enclosed him.

The bullet had struck his forehead directly below the rim of the steel helmet.

13

The American's death was the final straw for Scholten. He heard Mutz weeping silently beside him, and he felt that unless something happened, he too would soon be in tears. He looked over to Hager and noticed with sudden dismay that he had taken hold of Horber's shoulders, and was shaking him back and forth. He saw Horber rolling over on his back. Horber's right hand slipped down from his belt, and fell limply to the stone slabs of the pavement, in the middle of a puddle.

The hand lay there, yellow and lifeless. You're dreaming, he told himself. It can't be true. Horber dead? Christ! Horber, it isn't true! You were so happy only last night! You still sat here with us, only a while back . . .

And Scholten thought further: You can't know how touched I was, a few hours ago, when I saw you weep. It was the first time I ever saw you weep, and now you're dead!

He nudged Mutz. "They got him, Albert," he said, and pointed to Karl Horber. Mutz turned his face to the other half of the bridge, then let his head sink down to his arms, and wept even more unrestrainedly. "Poor Mutz," Scholten thought, "that is too much even for you!"

The pity Scholten felt for the strong Mutz who cowered beside him and wept like a little boy spurred him on. Hager, over on the other side, was still trying to prop Horber up. He had seen the wound in Horber's forehead, but somehow he failed to grasp the implication of that ugly, gaping hole between Horber's eyes. Mechanically, he continued to prop up the lifeless body time and again, and to shake it by the shoulders. Scholten watched him, thinking: Unless I go over there, they'll get Hager too. That guy is sitting almost upright behind the wall; if he lifts his head up any higher, he's lost.

Scholten peered through the embrasure and surveyed the line of houses opposite him. Six, seven open windows, black holes. If there were any Americans there, they were in a splendid position. The safest possible cover. They could look out without being seen themselves.

Scholten knew if danger lurked for him, it could only come from these windows. The doors to the houses and the entrances to the courtyards he could see clearly. He threw a glance up to the rooftops of the nearest houses; they too seemed to be deserted.

And suddenly Scholten became aware of something. Something disquieting he felt all around him. And all at once he knew what it was. The stillness.

Not only had they stopped shooting, but the American guns too had become silent.

Can it be possible? Scholten thought. Could they have left?

"Mutz," he said. "Hey, Mutz, listen, don't you notice something?"

Mutz raised his head. From time to time he was still shaken by a sob. He listened. Then he turned his face to Scholten. A cautious smile passed over his dirt-splashed gray cheeks.

"They've gone, Ernst, they've stopped!"

Scholten and Mutz were overjoyed, but they didn't quite trust the peace as yet. Scholten wanted to be on the safe side.

"Here, Albert, take my rifle," he said. "Don't look after me when I start running. Just watch those open windows there. Aim at those windows right now. And if you see anything, shoot—shoot all you can!"

He grabbed the sten gun and held it out towards Mutz. But Mutz shook his head. "Don't be sore, Ernst, but I can't fire another shot. I don't want to any more. Not since this!" He pointed to the dead American in front of the house.

"O.K., Mutz," Scholten said after a brief pause. "I'll make a run for it, as is. It'll be all right!"

When Mutz saw that Scholten was serious about it, he obediently snatched up the rifle, pushed it through the embrasure, aimed the barrel up at the windows, pulled the butt back, and put his finger on the trigger.

"You've got to have a good grip on it, Mutz," Scholten whispered, "it has a strong pull upward."

It sounded cynical.

Scholten went into a crouch behind the stone projection, then bolted up and dashed over to Hager.

Mutz saw the flares in two windows, heard at the same time the ghastly bursts, and was tempted to turn his head around to look after Scholten. "Dear God," he prayed, "they mustn't get him too. Not him, not him . . . I'd sooner it was me!"

And as he was praying and wondering at the same time why he earnestly preferred to die himself rather than see Scholten killed, he pulled the trigger. He couldn't explain how he knew. But he knew that he had hit the mark.

At least the one in the left window. He was so sure of it that he stood up with the rifle, put the elbow of the supporting hand on the pile of stones, and from this exposed standing position fired at the second window. Then he saw again the flare in that window, heard the whistling sound, and felt a burning in his arm, even as he heard the whistling.

From the other side of the bridge, he heard Scholten yelling: "Lie down, you god-damn idiot!"

Thank God, Mutz thought, he screams, so he must be alive. Nothing has happened to him. He threw himself down behind the stone wall, heard a second bullet whistle past, and thought again: He's alive, nothing happened to him!

Then he looked over to Scholten. He saw him kneeling behind the breastwork and talking to Hager, gesturing vehemently with his hands. Hager cowered next to him as if drunk. He was swaying from side to side, and Scholten slapped his face now. With the flat of his hand, he slapped him right and left. Hager didn't understand. After a while, he seemed to come to himself again. He warded off one of Scholten's blows with his forearm as though he were saying: "That's enough!"

Ernst Scholten had had no alternative. When he reached the other side of the bridge, he found Hager sitting beside Horber and looking as though he had gone crazy.

"So that's how one looks when one goes mad," Scholten said. Hager was staring at him with wide-open, shining eyes. He sang: "Today Germany is ours, and tomorrow the whole world . . ."

It was then that Scholten struck him.

And he didn't stop viciously hitting him until Hager raised his elbow to cover his face.

"I'm sorry, Ernest," he said. "Please forgive me."

"That's all right," Scholten said. "Everyone cracks up sooner or later!" But he resolved to be on guard.

"It was Mutz first," he went on, "now it's you. In five minutes it might be me. I only beg you, Klaus, if it happens, beat me up, hit me as hard as you can until I say: 'Enough, Klaus, I'm O.K. now.' You know we can't afford to crack up now. Do you hear me?"

Scholten shoved the body aside, and lay down behind the machine gun.

"It's still in order," Hager said. "Nothing at all has happened to the gun." And he looked once again at Horber.

Scholten had made a note of the window from which the shots had been fired. He aimed at it, then motioned to Mutz.

"Come over," he yelled, "and bring the rifle with you."

Obediently, Albert took hold of the sten gun, slung his carbine over his shoulder, and crouched behind the stone wall. As soon as Scholten opened fire, he dashed across the bridge with giant leaps, and, breathing heavily, threw himself down alongside Scholten.

"Look, Ernst," he said, "there are only two Americans left up there, at the most. Or there would have been more shots. I got the one in the left window, but the other one is still there shooting away, and his aim isn't bad!"

Strange, Scholten thought, how one can sit around weeping one moment, and then when the time comes to do something, one is quite all right again.

"It was the one in the right window who just took a shot at you, Albert," he said. "There aren't any more, or they'd have had a go at you when you made a run for it. They have probably withdrawn, and left just a few scouts behind."

Scholten had said scouts, and Mutz was reminded of the times Scholten had played scout when they had gone on the warpath with air guns and wooden tomahawks.

Scholten had meanwhile continued: "If they did withdraw, it must have been for a reason. They are not through with us. They won't let us off that easy. We should try to get that guy up there, and then beat it the hell out of here. As long as he is there, not one of us can get away."

Mutz felt as if a load had been lifted from him when he heard his friend Scholten speak of beating it. Christ, he thought to himself, we're going to beat it. Of course we are going to beat it. We've held the bridge, we have done enough.

Mutz was worked up, his devil-may-care attitude had vanished. He burned with impatience as he helped Scholten think of the best way to go about it.

Scholten took his steel helmet off, put it on top of Hager's carbine and slowly raised it up. He had once seen a picture in which a soldier was shown raising his helmet over the trench to see, without endangering himself, if he'd draw fire. He could not remember exactly where he had seen it. Not that it matters right now, he thought.

As soon as the helmet showed a few inches above the

wall, a shot rang out, stone fragments flew around his ears, and Scholten pulled the helmet down again. He tried it again, while Mutz was aiming the sten gun at the window.

"I'm ready," he whispered excitedly, and Scholten pushed the helmet aloft. As soon as it was above the wall, there was again a *pffft* and *pengg* from the window, and the steel helmet was spinning and whirling around the barrel of the carbine.

Mutz had let loose a barrage of twenty shots, but he cursed now: "A tricky bastard, a damn tricky bastard!"

"You're so right, Mutz!" Scholten said. He scrutinized the little hole punctured through the front of the helmet. I wonder what sort of rifle he's using, Scholten thought. The one by the chestnut tree had carried a short one, but this hole seems to come from a larger caliber.

Then he noticed that the sleeve of Mutz's jacket was all red, that blood was trickling down his left hand, and that the sten gun had red splashes on it.

"Let's have a look at you," he said, frightened. Albert looked down at his arm, astonished. Here he was wounded, bleeding, the blood had even begun to form a little puddle on the ground, and he hadn't even noticed. Now he remembered the burning he had felt when he was aiming at the window and had seen the shot flare up, a while back. Well now, they got him, and he hadn't even noticed it.

He pushed the sleeve up with his right hand. Some two inches above the elbow was an ugly abrasion, partly still open, partly crusted over. Blood was oozing from it in two, three thick strands. Nothing to speak about, Albert Mutz thought, it hardly hurts. But suddenly he felt the pain when he moved his arm, and the wound throbbed. It should be bandaged, he thought, and heard Scholten cursing.

"Christ, the bandages! What idiots we are. Took everything along, rifles, bazookas, machine guns, even food, but the bandages we completely forgot."

"Fröhlich forgot them," Mutz corrected him. "Fröhlich or Heilmann!"

They both thought of Fröhlich and Heilmann now. Where could they possibly be? Did they get Fröhlich too, or had he been captured by the Amis? Had Heilmann really deserted them, or had he been detained somewhere? Was he perhaps lying behind some protective wall, the same as they, and waiting?

Scholten pulled out a big red striped handkerchief from his trouser pocket. He folded it to a narrow strip, bandaged the wound, made a knot and pulled tight.

"Ouch," Mutz said, feeling miserable, because it really hurt now.

"If any dirt gets into it, you can get lockjaw," Hager said, and stared at the bandage with interest. It was the first sentence he had spoken since Mutz had come over.

When they had finished bandaging the wound, Mutz rolled the damp sleeve of his jacket down again, and Scholten pointed to the window. "Let's try it once again," he said, "before the tanks come back and we don't stand a chance."

He took the helmet with the punched hole, and put it on Hager's carbine. He gave Hager the rifle. "You hold it up," he said.

Then he lay behind the machine gun, and aimed it at the window. Mutz pressed the sten gun against his shoulder. They both stared across. Hager hoisted the helmet aloft.

Pffft, pengg. The helmet spun around the carbine. Scholten and Mutz fired the guns. But they soon quit in disgust.

"He's too damn fast for us," Scholten said, and bit his lip. "We'll never get that guy!"

As if the American had noticed what they'd been up to, a steel helmet now appeared in the window. It was raised so high that they could clearly see it had been hoisted aloft on a broomstick or a pole.

The stick swung to and fro, the helmet jiggling. This was adding insult to injury. "Look at that son of a bitch," Scholten said, not without admiration. "Unless we get him, we'll never get out of here."

Hager opened his mouth. "I'll just dash over to the other side," he said. "You may have better luck that way."

He was trembling with excitement. He cowered against the wall and was just about to take off, when Scholten seized him by the scruff of the neck.

"Looks like you already forgot the beating you took a little while back, you mad dog," he said. "What do you think this is? A kindergarten? Aren't three heroes enough for you?" He pushed him roughly so that he fell against the wall. "I'm going to keep my eyes on you, son," Scholten threatened. "You try that again, and I'll beat you to a pulp. Do you understand?"

Hager cowered against the wall and wiped the blood from his cheeks. He must have brushed the stones as he fell back. He said not a word. But his eyes shone wildly and wandered from one to the other.

"Mutz," he said then, "don't you think I'm right? We'll never get that bird any other way. We do want to get out of here. I'll just run over to the other side of the bridge. I'll stop there. Then I'll go on to the chestnut tree, stop again. And then I'll make a run for the house. He'll have to come out of the window then if he wants to get me."

"Beautiful, Hager," Scholten said. "A first-rate scheme. You just forgot one minor detail. You might never even make it across the bridge."

Scholten and Mutz again turned their attention to the window. "How in hell are we going to get that bird?" Scholten wondered. "There must be some trick we haven't tried yet," Mutz said.

"How about giving the helmet routine another try," Scholten said, and pressed the carbine into Hager's hand. Then he lay down behind the machine gun, and Mutz adjusted the rifle to his shoulder. Both stared across. It was just what Hager had been waiting for.

He thrust the carbine with the helmet aside, shot up and dashed across the bridge, puffing like a steam locomotive.

Pffft, pffft, pengg. Twice, a flare lit up the window. "Fire, Mutz!" Scholten screamed. "Fire, don't turn around!"

He let the machine gun sputter, and Mutz added to it the fire from the sten gun. The lanky Hager had made it. He was lying behind the stone projection on the other side of the bridge, gasping for air. He bolted up and raced to the chestnut tree.

Pffft, it came again. Scholten and Mutz fired, and Hager stood behind the huge treetrunk, recovering his breath.

"I think we've got him," Mutz said. "Hell, we've got him," Scholten replied, and sent desperate signals to the chestnut tree. Hager better stop, he thought. He'd better not take another step.

But Hager had merely paused for breath, as planned, and now ran straight to the house in which the American had entrenched himself.

KLAUS HAGER AND THE FEAR OF LIFE

Hager had never attracted much attention. As far back as they could remember, he had always just been there, without ever making himself conspicuous. Hager prefers to remain in the background, the others thought. He is a decent chap, glad to be left alone, in peace. They couldn't have been more wrong!

"How often must I tell you not to sit down at the table with dirty hands?" That was his mother.

Klaus Hager had to wash his hands before every meal. So did Mutz for that matter, and Forst and all the rest. Only Klaus had been told it too often to be able to go to a faucet without aversion. When he was a little boy of six, or seven, he sat down to lunch with unwashed hands, day after day. Sometimes there were slaps, other times he was simply sent to wash up, but on occasion his mother forgot to check. On those days Hager felt triumphant.

"Don't bring all these dirty animals into the house!"

Klaus could not see a cat, a bird, a lizard, or even a mouse, without it stirring a desire in him to catch the beast and take it home. Fortunately these expeditions were seldom successful. His mother would have despaired otherwise; all animals disgusted her. Once Klaus caught a little blackbird whose wings had been injured. Cautiously, he put the bird in a box, and sat up half the night tenderly caring for his little patient. When he awoke next morning, his first thought was of the bird. He climbed out of bed, ran barefoot to the little box, and found it empty.

For half an hour, he searched the room until he found the blackbird. It was lying under a cupboard. The little body was already stiff. Klaus Hager was so desperate, emitting the most heart-rending sobs, that his parents were seriously worried about him.

His father bought him a parakeet. "Here you've got another sweet little bird now." But Klaus knit his brows fiercely. "I don't want a sweet little bird!" He screamed and stamped his feet. "I want my blackbird again!"

He buried the bird in the garden and on the little grave put a stone slab which his father had inscribed, and then stuck a little wooden cross beside it. Many children had done the same before him, many a child will do so after him. But the death of the little blackbird cast a shadow over the spirits of the little boy for so long a time that his parents were alarmed. They anxiously kept from him all influences they considered harmful, and let him start school a year later. On the first morning in school, Hager stood alone in the schoolyard during recess. After a while, he did find some friends, but only found them to quarrel with them.

Once he came home with torn socks. They had beaten him up because he had snitched on his neighbor. "My dear little boy," his mother said tearfully, "what have they done to you?" She felt so sorry for little Klaus that at last he began to weep himself. When his father came up and saw what was going on, he had an argument with his wife, much to the boy's astonishment. "Don't spoil the brat," his father said, "he isn't a little girl. For heaven's sake, try to understand that, Emily." But Emily

Hager didn't understand, and from that day on, his father had to call for Klaus at school, every day exactly at noon.

Klaus got excellent report cards. After some deliberation, his parents decided to let him enter high school after only three years of public school, instead of the usual four. This way he made up for the lost year, and started high school with children his age. He was quiet and attentive in class, never laughed or talked during the hour, and actually was rather well liked. The tendency to snitch on others had been knocked out of him in public school. He usually hung around Mutz, Scholten and Forst, and they took him along. They never spoke roughly to him, and in some ways he received even more consideration than little Siegi Bernhard. They always made it a special point to ask him along on their expeditions.

"What say, Hager, coming to the beach this afternoon?"

Mutz and Scholten had put the question to Hager. Hager was coy. "Oh, I don't really know yet, you usually go too fast for me, and then my bike seems to be on the blink, well I just don't know . . ."

"All right, all right," Scholten interrupted him. "Mutz will walk home with you and ask your mother if you can come!"

Hager, suddenly transformed, no longer uncertain: "Would you really, Mutz? Well. Then I'll come of course. I'd love to come."

Hager was mostly not allowed to go, but when the reliable Mutz asked his mother, there was a chance. Hager never wanted to admit that. He had all sorts of excuses, until they got tired of them. It was mostly Scholten who interrupted the dilly-dallying and assured Hager shortly that one of them would be by to get Emily Hager's permission.

On one occasion, Scholten himself went, but the permission was not granted that day.

"Tell me, Klaus," his mother asked, "who is this disagreeable boy with the black hair and the yellow face? Is he in your class? What sort of grades does he get? Probably tells smutty stories, doesn't he? But of course you wouldn't tell me what nasty things you contrive!"

"You're wrong about him, Mama," Klaus bravely interrupted. "Really you are. I know him well. Honestly!"

"Well, if you stick up for him like that, there is sure to be something rotten somewhere," his mother said, and decided to find out more about Scholten. She went to see *Studienrat* Stern, to tell him all about Scholten. "An obstinate rascal," she said, "you just have to look into his eyes.

"I tell you, a born criminal," she whispered. "And someone like that is allowed to be in the same class as my boy!"

After Emily Hager left Stern's office, he took a few deep breaths, and thought: Poor Klaus!

Klaus Hager was average in everything he undertook. Nothing extraordinary was ever expected of him. But one morning his mother found him in bed, unconscious. The doctor was summoned, and he arranged for an immediate transfer to the hospital. Klaus's stomach was pumped out just in time. The dose of sleeping pills he had helped himself to, from his mother's night table, would have been sufficient for the whole family.

His mother stormed to school. "You are to blame," she reproached the teachers, "you asked too much from my boy."

"You are to blame," she challenged her husband. "You haven't taken enough of an interest in the boy!"

"No one is to blame," Klaus himself had written on a little slip of paper. "I just don't want to go on."

"Don't be hard on him, don't ridicule him, but don't be overly nice to him either," Stern cautioned his class. "Try and be casual about it, and he will find himself in no time at all again. There are times in life, children, when one blacks out. We have to do what we can for Klaus, only we must not let on to him."

"My dear lady," Stern said to Emily Hager, "try for once not to pin the blame on others. Try for once to be a sensible mother. It's all the same to me what you accuse us of. I do care about the boy. He won't slip up a second time, you can be sure of that!"

"A second time?" Emily Hager paled, and on her way home from school came close to examining her relationship with her son. But she only came close to it. *Studienrat* Stern went to the principal to acquaint him with Hager's case.

The principal, a gentle, kindly old man, listened in silence. "What he needs is a friend, colleague," he said at last. And when Stern, somewhat uncertainly, repeated: "A friend, sir?" the principal explained: "Yes, a friend. A boy, or better still a girl. He needs someone to take his mind off himself. One would have to entrust him with something, or someone helpless, in need of protection, something to arouse a feeling in him of being needed, of . . ."

"Isn't that a little . . ." Stern hesitated, not knowing how to put it, but saying anyway, "dangerous?"

It wasn't exactly what he had meant to say. But the principal had understood.

"That would very much depend on the girl, Stern!"

He had in mind a newcomer to the school, a shy little girl whose parents had enrolled her only two days before. She was to start classes the coming Monday.

Undoubtedly the girl would have a hard time making friends. But could one risk such an experiment? Wasn't there a danger that the whole thing might boomerang, and have the effect least desired?

"You'll have to be very careful, my friend," the principal said. Long after Stern left, the principal sat thinking about the whole affair. Wouldn't it be so much simpler to let Klaus shift for himself, swim along with the class? The principal looked up to the bust of Pestalozzi, which stood dusty and inconspicuous on top of the high, oak bookcase. To teach is to love, he thought— even though it would be so much easier to simply teach.

The new girl came on Monday. The class took absolutely no notice of her. It was always the same. "After all, one can't run after a silly little goose like that." Quietly, she sat in her place, a colorless little creature. She came from the east. Her parents had fled when the front lines were coming closer. Her two brothers were in the army. *Studienrat* Stern took down all her personal data. Her name was Franziska Feller. She was born in 1929. Stern asked her about her religion, her father's profession, and at the end told her to see him after class.

At the sound of the bell, the class stormed out into the schoolyard. Stern and little Franziska stayed in the room. He asked her what grades she had been getting. Then he said: "By and large, you should have no difficulty keeping up with the class, only your poor mark in Latin worries me. I'll ask a fellow student to help you a little with Latin."

The pretext had been found to bring Klaus Hager and Franziska Feller together.

Klaus Hager was sensitive. He knew it, but couldn't help it. He didn't know what made him that way, or what would arouse his sensitivity.

Once he witnessed a military funeral. The commander of the barracks, an old colonel, had died. Crowds of people lined the streets to the cemetery in the late afternoon, Klaus among them. Deeply moved, he watched the funeral procession: soldiers in long coats, with blackened helmets and tight chin straps that made their faces appear even more severe; a military band, playing a funeral march; behind it the gun carriage on which the coffin rested beneath a black sheet, and more soldiers. Endless gray columns. A gloomy, somber, disquieting scene. Klaus Hager felt a lump in his throat through it all. The music stopped, and only the muffled beats of a drum accompanied the steps of the marching men.

Long after the procession had passed, he stood still on the street. The spectators had dispersed. Far off he heard a trumpet, then the gun salute. When the columns returned, people rushed out of their houses. Some in the upper stories threw their windows open, and leaned far out. The men who had only just now marched by with slow, ominous tread, returned from the cemetery to the sound of drums and trumpets. Songs rose up from the gray columns. The companies marched past with resounding step. Drums boomed, fifes whistled, and the men broke out into a loud song:

> The sun gleams red, be ready men;
> Who knows if tomorrow she'll shine for us again . . .

"It's the song of the parachutists," an old lady next to Klaus said, and he felt the tears coming into his eyes. Suddenly, he too wanted to march with the men. There was something about all this—he could not explain. But this was only one aspect of his sensitivity.

Klaus Hager loved to kneel in church on Sundays. Strange, he thought every now and then with troubled conscience, I go to church, but I can't pray. He was always in time for the service. He knelt in his pew, tried to say the Lord's Prayer, but suddenly his thoughts would soar upward to the dome, carried aloft by the rousing sounds of the organ and the jubilation of the chorus. He gloried in the atmosphere of the place, heightened by the incense, the burning candles, and the number of devout worshipers.

He loved best to stand in a dark corner of the church during the May devotion; when the high female voices and the deep male basses rose in unison, praising the Queen of Heaven in glorious, beautiful hymns, Klaus gave himself up completely to that mystical enchantment that touched everything within. Often he stood before the small niche of the Mater Dolorosa. When the last rays of the evening sun transfigured the austere countenance of the statue, there was a fixed staring look in his eyes, and a sense of wonder, a feeling of painful ecstasy shuddered through his body.

Once he confessed that he could not pray in church, that he could only just sit and listen to what went on inside himself. "That is no sin," the priest said softly, and a smile appeared on his face. But Klaus Hager could not see that through the grating of the confessional.

Whenever Klaus felt that he had been unjustly treated at home, he went to bed early, lay quietly staring up at the ceiling and thought: I am gravely ill, I will die. They'll carry me to the cemetery, and everyone will gather around my grave. My mother and father, the teachers and the class. They'll weep, and remember how often they had wronged me.

He saw himself lying in the coffin, a pale, smiling face, surrounded by flowers.

As he got to know Franziska better, that changed. He thought less of dying, and could no longer understand that he had ever been prompted to reach for the sleeping pills. If they had found me half an hour later, I might be dead now, he thought with dread—they'd have forgotten all about me by now.

Klaus Hager did not suffer from the physical tensions that troubled other boys his age. Nor did he have the disquieting dreams that turned their nights into a torture. The difficulties of his age came to the fore in a morbid emotionality, a sickly impressionableness whenever he was subjected to any moving experience. Music could do this to him. Though he was incapable of learning an instrument himself, he could sit enraptured for hours before the phonograph, listening to the symphonies of Brahms and Tchaikowsky, Mendelssohn's violin concerto, and the piano concertos by Rachmaninoff.

It wasn't always that a given mood drove him to his record collection. Far more often, he consciously created the mood, and then worked himself up to such a pitch of intensity that his mother frequently found him sitting in tears beside the record player. It was like a poison, a sweet, intoxicating poison. And Emily Hager did not turn the record player off, as any other mother would have done after the second or third time. Instead she bent over her son, stroked his hair with her hand. He is as sensitive as I am, she thought with a mixture of sadness and pride.

The fear that his friendship with Franziska would stir

137

up feelings that had remained dormant until now proved unfounded. But another danger took its place. Klaus Hager, sensing that something weak had come under his influence, developed into a veritable little tyrant. After two months, Stern began to consider how he might separate the two without upsetting Klaus's balance in undoing what Klaus had gained. A setback in one as sensitive as he could easily lead to another crisis. But something had to be done, Stern felt, whenever he looked at little Franziska in the morning, saw her sitting restless in her place, shy and ill at ease.

Klaus Hager was jealous. He practically regarded Franziska as his personal property. For it was she who cowered beside him in front of the Gramophone, who shared his wild outbursts with admiring attention, who looked up to him. But the problem Stern saw before him solved itself.

One evening Klaus Hager had to take an urgent letter to the station for his mother. She wanted to make sure that it would make the last train out. He took the letter to the mail coach, and, returning, saw Franziska on the platform alongside the car directly behind the locomotive. She was not alone. A young man in soldier's uniform stood next to her, bent down to her little face and kissed her. Then he ascended the three steps to his coach, laughing and waving with his left hand, and disappeared through the door. Franziska's hand was raised too; forlornly she held it up until the train started to move. Klaus Hager rushed past her. Franziska had seen him, and called out in surprise: "Klaus!" When he ran on, she called again tearfully: "Klaus, hey listen, don't run!"

Once again she waved to the young man who stood

smiling in the window of the compartment, waving a big, white handkerchief. Then she ran after Klaus. She caught up with him outside his house, talked to him. She was simply at a loss to understand what had happened. He stared at her with burning eyes—it made her heart sink—and said: "Go away!"

She left him.

Klaus Hager threw himself on the bed in his room, and sobbed. He thought again of the capsules in his mother's night table, and quietly stole into her room. That will teach her, he thought, that will really teach her a lesson. He reached his hand out for the drawer, when he heard his mother's voice. "No, you don't, Klaus. Not this time. I heard you coming in, and suspected something like this. Not because of some silly little girl, Klaus!"

Ashamed, he crawled back to his own room. His mother came in after him. "Why don't you listen to some music, Klaus?" she said softly. "That always seems to help you." He went to his record player, and put on Tchaikowsky's sixth symphony. His sensitive nature conjured up an orgy of painful, phantastic images.

A few days later he got the draft notice. Emily Hager ran to the family doctor, to the school, the municipality, to the draftboard, and to party headquarters. Finally she realized that she was up against something over which she had no control.

For the first time Klaus felt sorry for his mother—and he also felt sorry for himself, and for the whole world, in fact. With tears in his eyes, he left home.

In the barracks, the boys showed no consideration for his sensitivity. There was no mother to help, and no Franziska to look up adoringly at him. Once in those fourteen days, he told Mutz about what had happened.

"You big oaf," Mutz said in a friendly way. "I also saw Franziska that evening. She was bringing her brother to the station!"

Hager was crushed. He begged Schaubeck for a pass to go into town. "What business have you got in town?" Schaubeck foamed with rage. "At your age you don't need a dame yet!" Hager resigned himself.

Two days before the alarm, he had a chance to go home. He briefly saw his folks, then went to Franziska's house. But she sent word that she wasn't home. He heard her say so to her mother, who came down and said, embarrassed: "Franziska isn't well, she's in bed!"

Hager returned to the barracks, and kept even more to himself, was even more inconspicuous than ever. His disappointment stuck like a thorn in him, and it gave him a perverse pleasure to touch it till it hurt. One day I'll do something big, he dreamed. I'll do something extraordinary, and I'll be killed in the process, but they'll remember the deed.

On the bridge, he was scared at first, then became indifferent. Siegi's death, and later on Jürgen's, unnerved him. And when he saw Horber lying dead beside him, he said to himself: I am going out of my mind, I am going out of my mind!

When Scholten struck him, as one strikes a drunken man to wake him out of his stupor, he came to himself and was ashamed. And in his shame, he swore anew that he'd do something bold, that he'd show them: I'm not a milksop, I'm not a mama's boy—just you wait and see!

When Hager had reached the other side of the bridge, he felt everything becoming light and free about him. What will you do when you reach the house? he asked himself, and discovered that he had no weapon other than his bayonet.

He drew the bayonet from the scabbard, and made straight for the house. He saw an olive-green figure in the window, and jumped aside. Running on, he turned his head, shouting over his shoulder: "Shoot, shoot, here he is!"

He did not hear the shot coming from the window, nor did he see the flash. Abruptly, he was stopped by an enormous thrust against his breast. As he keeled over and darkness surrounded him, the last sound he heard was the furious hammering of the machine gun.

They've got him, he thought. I've done it.

They had indeed gotten him. Scholten hit him as he was about to put a second slug into Hager. For a moment the American leaned on the window sill, then he sank slowly back into the room. The rifle remained on the window sill, the barrel pointing somewhere into the distance.

Scholten got up. He was unspeakably tired. Then Mutz too raised himself. They stared across to the windows, then at Hager, who lay small and strangely twisted up in front of the line of houses.

His right hand was still clutching the bayonet.

14

"Come," Scholten said to Mutz, "let's go home!"

"Forst!" Mutz suddenly remembered. "He's probably still down below the bridge, waiting for tanks."

They looked out into every direction, then went down to Forst. He lay with half his body resting on a pile of bazookas, and they started back in horror for a moment. Was he also . . . ?

But when they came closer, they were dumbfounded to find Walter snoring away softly. He was fast asleep.

He had been sleeping right through the skirmish above. Scholten kicked him in the side.

"Wake up, you bum," he said gruffly. Forst stretched himself, yawned sleepily, and finally opened his eyes.

He was still on his back, looking up surprised at Scholten and Mutz. Suddenly his face lit up: "Kids, I've been sleeping the war away." He jumped to his feet.

"Let's go," Scholten said. "It's high time we beat it."

"Where are the Amis?" Forst asked.

"Gone," Scholten replied.

They heard planes. They wanted to get out from under the bridge, but there was no time. The air vibrated with the din of motors. Three Mustangs zoomed across, only about thirty feet above the bridge. They heard the *ack-ack* of the heavy machine guns, and the *braffz-braffz* of the parachute flares as they fell on the bridge.

"I hope they don't drop any bombs," Mutz whispered.

"Maybe we could get them with the machine gun," Forst suggested.

"Stay put," Scholten said and listened.

The planes returned, again opened machine-gun fire, and again they heard *braffz-braffz* resounding from the bridge above. Three more times the planes returned. Then the sound of the motors abated in the distance.

Scholten and Mutz climbed up the embankment to the bridge. Forst stumbled along after them. When he saw the dead, he was shocked speechless.

There were big holes in the road on the bridge, and traces of shell-fire were visible on the pavement and the railing. The machine gun Scholten had last used was a wreck. As if bent by a giant fist, the barrel stared straight up.

They looked once more up the road west, and Scholten said: "Let's go."

"And what about our orders?" Forst asked, disconcertedly.

"I shit on that," Scholten said fiercely. "There's a limit to everything. No one can order me to stay on until I'm killed. And what if I get killed, what's that going to help? We were told to hold the bridge, and we did hold it. Four of us fell, what more?"

Forst said: "I'll do whatever you do, of course. You know that!" And Scholten thought of the General.

Did we actually carry out his order, he asked himself, or didn't we? If we didn't, then the General wanted nothing else from the beginning but that we fight on here until we are all killed.

Christ, in that case the General is responsible for those four over there. He can't have wanted that? That isn't possible, is it?

15

The General stood in the low room of the farmhouse and looked at his watch. Runners came in and out continuously, saluted, made their reports. The last dispatch said: "Division left square Caesar four, Berta two, in orderly fashion, and is now retreating to alternate positions. Rearguard in ordered strength left at the eastern rim of the town." The General breathed a sigh of relief. Suddenly, he became aware that beads of perspiration had formed on his forehead.

He pulled a handkerchief from the sleeve of his coat and wiped his face. Then he lifted his field cap and rubbed the handkerchief along his massive head down to the collar of his uniform. It worked, he thought. He felt the pride of the strategist whose calculations had proved accurate. He looked at his watch again, it was exactly five o'clock.

Another runner came in. He was from the observation post on the church tower. This was his message: "The reported American advance patrols have withdrawn after a brief exchange of fire before the bridge. Bridge held. Two enemy tanks destroyed."

By Jove, the General thought, the little devils. For a moment he saw the faces of the boys before his eyes, but only in a blur. The General had seen too many faces to remember details.

It all had come about as he had anticipated. The Americans had sent a strong advance patrol, had received fire, had withdrawn in orderly fashion. Clearly, the General could foresee the next move. Bombers, artillery, a patrol, and then again bombers, artillery, a patrol, until that patrol would relay the word: The bridge is no longer being held!

In just this way, the Americans had been pushing back the German units ever since they had crossed the borders. A devilish sort of strategy this. One especially designed to save the lives of their own soldiers. Again and again; planes and artillery until the German soldiers were smoked out of their foxholes, and, exhausted, left them to fall back a few miles and dig in anew. Then planes, artillery, planes, artillery . . .

Another runner came. The observation post on the church tower reported: "Three enemy bombers, Mustangs, attacking the bridge with machine guns and parachute flares. No bombs. That is all!"

The General saw again the blurred faces of the boys before his eyes, and then recalled the report. "No bombs," it had said.

Of course, the Americans want the bridge whole. The General looked at his watch again. Six minutes past five. He sent for the Lieutenant of the demolition squad that had been waiting outside the farmhouse since noon for reassignment.

"Hampel," the General said, "we can still upset the American applecart. We'll blow the bridge up. Take six men, and get going. Be careful, Hampel, there may be bombers around. Possibly, by now, tanks too!"

Hampel saluted, and was ready to leave. Before he reached the door, the General said: "Just a moment, Hampel. Tell the boys on the bridge they can go home."

"Yes, Herr General!" Hampel was about to go again, when the General's voice held him back a second time: "One more thing, Hampel. Tell the boys that I am proud of them!"

He said it as though he could justify himself that way. Then he got ready to break camp. Outside, he realized that he had forgotten something. He went back, opened the drawer of the heavy table, and took out of it his wife's picture in a thin, silver frame. A pity, the General thought as the boys came to his mind again, a pity we haven't any children!

And he was suddenly struck by the thought: Would you have given this order if your son had been one of them? The General slipped the picture into his pocket. Strange, he thought, desperately trying to forget the seven on the bridge, after three years in Russia I am suddenly becoming sentimental!

16

The three on the bridge were determined to leave.

"You walk ahead," Walter Forst said. "I'm coming right away, I only want to stow some of the bazookas away to make sure nothing happens down there." He waved them on. Scholten slung the sten gun around his shoulder, Mutz took his carbine, and the two together crossed the bridge to the eastern bank and waited.

There followed a burst and an explosion. Heavy smoke rose up to the left and right of the bridge, pungent white-gray fumes, and then the air pressure hit them. Scholten and Mutz ran back, stumbled, fell, slid down the embankment through layers of white smoke, and shouted:

"Walter, what happened, where are you?"

But they received no answer.

Actually, no one really liked him. He was stocky, but did not seem heavy. His manner was self-assured, but cold and impersonal. Walter couldn't remember ever being ordered to do things at home by anyone, with the exception of the *Standartenführer,* whose orders he defied on principle and with unconcealed scorn. He might have become a youth leader, he had the qualifications for it. But the fact that it might have pleased the *Standartenführer* was reason enough to spurn any such offer. He hated his father, always had, as far back as he could remember. His father was a staunch party man who displayed towards his superiors an assiduous, hypocritical civility, and towards his subordinates a brutality bordering on sadism. His wife, Walter's mother, he treated worst of all.

Walter heard many times in school what people like his father were called. Not infrequently, at their get-togethers, Walter pulled a dusty bottle of fine old burgundy out of his pocket and placed it on the table, saying: "Here is a bottle of big shot wine!" In this respect Walter Forst was very reliable. His comrades knew that and valued it. One could sound off about the Hitler Youth in his presence, and tell the latest political jokes —which, by the way, was about the extent of their political discussions. Walter Forst himself was the expert on the Nazi philosophy of "purity and beauty" as it applied to the girl youth movement. Hardly a day passed on which he did not have a new group of dirty jokes.

Once, when they were studying Goethe's *Urfaust* in class, Walter had to read the part of Mephistopheles. He read the part so convincingly that it sent shivers down the spines of his fellow students. For a while they called him Mephisto, a name he rather liked. But they dropped it, for Walter could sing different tunes as well. He was the best reader in the class, and his recitation of Goethe's "Prometheus" was the high point of every school performance. Walter was the only one in his class who took a closer and more critical interest in the government. But in passing judgment on the government, he was actually passing judgment on his father. And he hated it, as he hated his father.

One experience was indelibly imprinted on his mind. It happened on an evening in November, in 1938, when he was nine years old. In his immediate vicinity lived the Freundlichs. They had only a small store, but it seemed to do well. Abi Freundlich, their son, who was the same age as Walter, was always well dressed. The parents were self-respecting and respected by others. Abi Freundlich—his full name was Abraham—was one of Walter's very best friends. They visited each other frequently and played together. Walter and Abi spent many afternoons in Abi's room setting up his big electric train.

The two boys were playing in Walter's house one day when the *Standartenführer* came home surprisingly early. Walter heard excited voices in the living room; his parents were quarreling. One sentence of his father's he could make out distinctly: "How many times do I have to tell you this! We can't let our son have a Jew boy for a friend!"

Forst looked at little Abi. "Is it true that you're a Jew?" he asked, surprised.

The nine-year-old Abi swallowed and bravely held the tears back. Then he nodded and ran out of the house. He never came back after that, and Walter Forst was strictly forbidden to visit him.

The *Standartenführer* had forbidden it, but Walter still spent afternoons in the apartment of his Jewish friend. When his father questioned him, he lied boldly and with assurance. This went on until that rainy afternoon in November 1938.

He had heard his parents quarreling again. This was after they had finished eating, and Walter had gone to his room to read an exciting book about Indians. Suddenly he heard his father's cold, brutal voice, raging mad, and then his mother's high-pitched voice, cracking as she shrieked: "Don't expect me to go along with this filthy business!" Doors were slammed. The *Standartenführer* had gone out.

Seconds later the door to Walter's room opened. His mother held a slip of paper on which a few lines were scribbled, and she was putting it into an envelope. Walter looked at his mother, she was horribly pale.

"I know it's late, Walter," she said. "But why don't you run over to Abi Freundlich and play there a little while?"

"You know he's forbidden it, Mutti," Walter said, surprised. "He'll notice it if I go this late!"

"That won't make any difference today," his mother said. "It's very important that you go. Do you understand? It's for your friend's sake. You must give this letter to his mother! The rest will work out!"

Although Walter did not really understand why his mother was making all this fuss about a ridiculous letter, he obediently took his raincoat and ran over to the Freundlichs. Papa Freundlich opened the door. Walter handed him the letter and said: "My mother sends this to you with her regards!"

Old man Freundlich looked at the letter, then at Walter, who finally asked if he could go up to Abi for a while. "Why, of course," Papa Freundlich laughed. "He'll be happy to see you."

Walter ran up the stairs to Abi's room. They set the train up and played. Outside in the hall there was a continuous back and forth, and once Abraham's mother put her head into the children's room and said: "Abi, come out here for a minute!"

Walter Forst went on playing by himself. Then little Abraham came back into the room. He was wearing his coat and his cap, and behind him stood his parents, also fully dressed and ready to go out. In their hands they held bags, rucksacks, and umbrellas.

"Give our best to your mother," old Freundlich said, and Abraham's mother gave Walter a kiss. Walter turned away, embarrassed. He hated it when strangers became affectionate and petted or kissed him. Then Abraham stood in front of him, his gray eyes old and serious beyond his years.

"We have to leave," he said. "You can have the train."

They went out. Walter rushed down the stairs after them. "Really, Abi?" he shouted. "Is it really mine?"

"Don't come along, don't shout, you must be quiet, very quiet," old man Freundlich said. "The train is yours, my boy. Now go on and pack it up. Take it right home with you before someone else comes and takes it away. Run along, my boy. Run along!" The Freundlichs headed down the street. Abi and Walter waved to each other until the fog swallowed up the fugitives. Walter went back to Abi's room as if he were at home there.

The nine-year-old knelt beside his train, and surveyed the treasure that had suddenly become his property. He pulled switches, turned the transformer on, worked the signals, let an express train with a black engine rattle down the yard-long track. In the last possible moment he prevented a crash, shifted points and was so completely absorbed in his playing that he forgot where he was.

He did not hear the heavy boots stomping up the stairs. He first heard the men when they were already in the hallway. "Where are you, Freundlich, you old *goniff*," a deep voice droned through the hall.

Walter cowered beside his train, frozen with fear. It was the voice of the *Standartenführer* . . .

He heard someone else say: "Seems the bird has flown the coop!"

The door to the children's room opened, a head with a brown cap peered in and shouted back: "They left the boy, *Standartenführer!*"

"That's something at least," Walter heard his father say, and then the *Standartenführer* stood in the doorway. "Good evening," Walter said, smiling timidly, and felt the first blow burning his cheek.

"But he gave me the train," Walter protested, crying. His father, red with rage, the swollen veins showing on his forehead, went on beating him mercilessly. He did not let off beating him until the boy lay on the floor beside the train, bleeding from his nose, mouth and ears.

"That was my son, men," he said. "Take a look at him!" Then they left. Later on a man in brown uniform came, and carried the quietly sobbing boy home.

That night, Walter's mother waited up for the *Standartenführer* a long time. He was drunk when he came in. As he took his coat off downstairs, he pushed the maid, who had opened the door, so hard in the chest she stumbled back against the wall. Then he staggered up the stairs to the living room, his thumbs stuck in the belt of his uniform.

"A fine son you've got," he barked at his wife. "Playing with Jews, embarrassing his own father! Who warned the Freundlichs?"

He was only two steps away from his wife, a head taller than she. But she stood her ground. "I warned them— and if you ever lay hands on the boy again, I'll kill you! I'll kill you, you big coarse beast—you, you scum!"

"You say that again, and I'll have you in jail!" the *Standartenführer* screamed.

"Maybe," she replied softly, but it sounded like a threat.

"Maybe," she said. "But you'll go there too. I made sure about that. I'm not as dumb as you think. My lawyer knows everything, the documents are in his safe, and he'll send them off the moment anything happens to me, or you so much as touch a hair on the boy's head. My lawyer is a party member! Now have me arrested, if you dare!"

She left the room. The *Standartenführer* rang for the maid, and asked for cognac, a whole bottle. When she brought him the bottle, he filled his glass and pulled her down to his lap.

Walter was in bed. He had heard his parents' quarrel from his room. I hate him, he thought, oh, how I hate him, and fell asleep.

Although he loved his mother and tried to show her his love, she saw to her sorrow that the boy was capable of changing within seconds from a nice child into a veritable little Satan. He felt sorry afterwards, and couldn't understand why others were not willing to forget his wrongdoings as quickly as he.

For hours he stalked through the garden of the house with his air rifle, shooting at the birds from close up.

There was a sinister gleam in his eye whenever he hit one, and saw the poor little feathered body falling dead to the ground as the rest of the flock scattered in all directions.

Once his aim had been off, and a little blackbird he had shot at came fluttering down, tweeted, and dragged its wing round and round in a circle. Walter tried to hit the bird again, but he kept missing until the janitor walked up with a big stick and smashed the bird's skull with one blow.

There was a faint creaking sound. The sound bored into Walter's ears and grew to a loud din. He ran up the terrace, took his rifle and smashed it to pieces. Then he ran to his mother and wept. And she thought: He is good at the core, my boy. Indeed there is both good and bad in every man, only his father is rotten through and through . . .

As Walter grew older his cruelty diminished; his capacity for hatred and malice gave way to a studied, rigid politeness. He was a boy one could not easily warm up to. It might have been because he could with one cynical comment torpedo the most pleasant conversation among friends. Or because he managed to impute a double meaning to almost anything that was being said.

The scoffers, to be sure, were on his side, but that was all. They didn't overly care for him, and Walter had few illusions on that score. The way he deliberately offended some who came to him in a friendly spirit gave the impression that Walter wanted to be feared, as though that, too, was in him and had to be let out.

It was the Führer's birthday. The classes assembled in the auditorium. The principal made the usual, meaningless speech. The radio was turned on and students as well as teachers listened, more or less attentively, to the broadcast.

Stern noticed the smell first. "It stinks," he said to the department head.

"I beg your pardon, colleague," the gentlemen said, perplexed.

"You misunderstand me," Stern said, smiling. "It stinks in here."

Others could smell it too by now. It was hydrogen sulphide. No mistaking that smell. It was easily identified. The classes cleared the hall. They found three squashed test tubes, and the cork stoppers to go with them, where the sixth grade had been standing.

Siegrun Bauer, the girls' gym teacher, demanded an investigation. The class remained silent, although the culprit couldn't have put the test tubes down unobserved. The entire class stood under suspicion, at least all the boys. There was only one exception. Walter Forst, son of the *Standartenführer*. But he was the one who had done it.

Stern did not pursue the investigation with all the necessary vigor, and he was frequently chided for it. "I have absolutely no objection to your taking the matter in hand," he said to Miss Bauer, and regarded her closely through the thick lenses of his spectacles. She soon left him, for she always felt a little uneasy in his presence. Stern secretly called her "the exhibitionist," but was careful not to utter such a remark aloud.

Jürgen Borchart wasn't the only one who had returned to the shower room to retrieve a forgotten article, and stood startled before the girls' gym teacher. Walter Forst had the same experience. Only he didn't run out. He stayed put, and under his stare she soon stopped laughing. For seconds he lingered by the door, and looked at her.

When she screamed at him that he should go, he turned around and, without saying a word, left. He tried it again on the following day, at the same time, right after the last class. He heard the water running, but found the door locked. On the third day he went again, and also on the fourth; he kept it up a whole week long.

Finally Fräulein Bauer's eccentricity won the upper hand over the scare Walter Forst had given her. On the sixth noon Walter found the door open. He stepped in and looked at her calmly, said nothing and left again.

Two weeks later, Walter Forst and Fräulein Bauer went bathing at a nearby lake. By the time they returned that night, Walter Forst knew all he wanted to know. Two days later he had his fifteenth birthday.

And two weeks after that, Walter learned that the afternoon by the lake was not free of consequences. They met in the evening, on a bench behind the stadium. She was no longer hard and eccentric, but a frightened girl who had lost all her composure.

"You shouldn't have left the door open," Walter said callously and obstinately. When she exploded in a fit of desperation, he told her: "Say it was my father, everyone will believe that!"

She lifted a hand to strike him, but he gripped her wrist and held firm. Then he disappeared, laughing, into the dark night.

She went to the principal and confessed all. He sent for Forst, but Forst knew nothing about it.

"I'm dumbfounded, sir. Really!" he lied easily and convincingly.

"But what about the shower room?"

"That's true, sir. But she made it a point of never closing the door. I wasn't the only one who saw her. Ask some of the others!"

The principal did not ask the others.

There was no proof against Walter Forst. He pulled out of the affair in style, affecting the air of the innocent boy who'd been unjustly accused. Stern alone was convinced that Fräulein Bauer's story was true, and he asked for Walter Forst's expulsion from school. He was voted down. Fräulein Bauer was transferred, and a scandal was avoided. But the affair was much talked about in the taverns around town.

They were whispering about it in class too, naturally, and it had the effect of increasing the distance between Walter Forst and the rest. But they didn't despise him, they were far too conscious of his being way ahead of them in many things.

Walter was once tried in Youth Court because he had knocked a man down on the street, and had injured him by kicking him severely. No one knew how that had come about. Forst was excused from school for the duration of the pre-trial police examinations. He idled the time away at home, sitting listless around the house.

His interest was suddenly aroused when a strange woman came to live with them. She was an evacuee from one of the big cities that had been devastated by bombings, and was billeted in their house. Walter went to the station for her luggage and helped her to get settled in the house. From the first day on, he spent a great deal of time around the young blond woman. The *Standartenführer* too suddenly stayed home evenings, and showed great concern for his guest. It gave Walter the keenest pleasure to embarrass his father on these occasions.

158

Once the *Standartenführer* gave a party. Walter had sufficient advance notice of the event to acquire, through a contact he had, the latest jazz recordings from Switzerland.

Just as the *Standartenführer* was fondling the small hand of the slender, blond woman at his side, and launching into one of his tirades about final victory, Walter set the needle down on *American Patrol*. It was the latest hit by a major in the American army named Glenn Miller. Walter Forst turned the volume of the record player up as loud as he could, and slumped indolently into the easy chair beside the Gramophone.

After the first few notes the party fell silent. All listened. It's a pity Mama went to bed, she ought to see this, Walter thought, and waited. His father rushed into the room, foaming with rage. His hands were clenched into fists, his arms raised.

Calmly, Walter stood only a few feet away from him, his arms folded, his eyes hard as glass.

"Go ahead," he said to his father. "Go on and hit me if you dare!" The look on his face left no doubt as to what would happen if the *Standartenführer* hit him.

Silently, Walter left the room. The party broke up early. The *Standartenführer* ended the evening alone with a bottle of cognac. Then he felt his way along the dark hall to the room of the evacuee. He was reaching for the doorknob when his foot touched something soft blocking the threshold.

"Don't trip," Walter said and got up. He waited till his father left, then went to his own room. I wonder what kept me from going in myself, he thought.

At the trial in Youth Court Walter was acquitted. He repeated the story he had told the police during the hearings earlier. The stranger had accosted him in the street and had asked him to go into the bushes with him. Walter was smooth and self-assured. "The man came up to me, and he grabbed my arm. I felt threatened, and I also saw it as an insult to my honor as a German youth!"

That'll do the trick, Walter thought. It never fails. The man Walter had beaten up was a homosexual with a police record, and that decided it. Walter Forst failed to say that he wasn't the least bit afraid of the man. And he concealed that he was downright pleased when the man accosted him. He had been looking for an excuse to beat him up in cold blood.

He frequently sat with the evacuee in the garden, behind the house. Her name was Helga. He read to her from one of his books, and asked with concern what news she had had from her husband in the army. Every word he spoke to her was calculated to create an impression of himself as a naive, unspoiled boy. He played the part most winningly. And though he couldn't quite explain to himself why he had chosen this role, his success proved he had chosen well. One evening, when he shyly rapped on her door to ask if she had anything for him to read, Helga took a little time before answering: "Why don't you come in, Walter?"

He opened the door, and saw her sitting in a dressing gown before the mirror. She was brushing her long blond hair. As Walter came nearer she stood up, and her gown came apart. He let her believe that she had seduced him. He woke up later that night at her side, and heard her weeping. It made him feel ashamed. He left her room silently. They never spoke about it, and when she moved out a few days later—because she had found a better room, she said—he was glad.

He returned to school. The brawl he had been in gave him the reputation of being not only cold and without scruples, but of being physically strong as well. They shied away from him even more. Once Mutz passed a snapshot of his cousin around the class. A pretty thing of maybe fifteen, in a light summer dress.

Forst took one look at it and said knowingly: "She'll make a nice lay some day!" This was during a break between classes. Mutz said simply: "See you after school."

"O.K.," Forst said.

After the last hour the boys assembled on the playground. Mutz stripped down to a pair of trunks. Forst did the same. Four schoolbags were used to circle off the ring.

"Boxing?" Forst asked.

"Anything you say," Mutz replied.

Then he went for Forst. First Mutz took a few jabs, but he soon had Forst in a clutch. Mutz turned abruptly about and stepped on Forst's foot. Walter hit the floor with a bang. Mutz waited for him to get up again, feinted a left straight to the jaw, while jabbing a right to Forst's stomach. Forst went down on his knees, gasping for air.

Mutz waited. From a crouching position Forst jumped at him. His forearm hit Mutz in the groin. Mutz spit, had to vomit, and in the same instant received a punch that sent him to the floor. He was so enraged that he was close to tears, but he checked himself. Slowly he got up from the floor and waited for Forst to charge anew. He held his right hand wide and loose to cover himself, but he withdrew it suddenly and lifted his knee with full force. At the same time he landed a left hook under Walter's jaw. Walter fell flat on the floor, rolled over once, and lay there dazed.

It took a few minutes to bring him around. He couldn't stand up straight, and had to be supported to walk.

"Care to tell me now what you think of my cousin?" Albert Mutz asked softly.

"She's a fine girl," Forst groaned.

Then he did something which immediately restored to him the respect of the class. As they walked off side by side, Forst suddenly stopped and spontaneously offered Mutz his hand. "Let's forget it, Mutz?" he asked. "Already forgotten, Forst!"

The whole class was assigned to do farmwork in the summer. Stern had to go along. On the first evening, the boys stood around the village pond and chatted. Forst was smoking a cigarette. Suddenly a truck pulled up alongside. A man in brown uniform got out, walked over to Forst and struck him in the face so that the cigarette fell out of his mouth. In a glowing arc the cigarette fell into the pond.

Forst hit back immediately. If the troopleader had taken him to task for smoking, he'd have thrown the cigarette away at once. But this wordless attack made Walter see red. His first punch split the upper lip of the uniformed man, and he was bleeding.

"Stop it, Walter," Mutz shouted, and wanted to hold his arm. "Think of the uniform!"

But Forst was infuriated. "I shit on his uniform," he said, and again went for the troopleader. He'd have killed him if his six friends hadn't all together pulled him away.

Walter was gone the following morning. By the time the *Bannführer* searched the house of the hop farmer, Walter was already sitting in his father's study.

"Just tell me how I'm to get you out of this one," his father fumed. "Something like this can break my neck and yours!"

"You have experience in these matters," Walter replied, unruffled. "Or am I mistaken?"

He was not mistaken. The *Standartenführer* was able to hush up this matter too.

After the holidays they met again in school, as though nothing had happened. But even Stern no longer knew what to make of Forst.

Forst had come to him one day: "There is something afoot, Herr Professor. Some big shot has it in for you. They want to draft you!"

Stern looked at him, inquiringly: "Why are you telling me this?"

"I don't like filthiness. I mean this sort of filth." Forst grinned.

There was no doubt in Stern's mind as to the sort of filth Walter did like.

"Well . . . Thank you anyway, Walter," Stern said.

"Don't mention it," Forst replied, and left.

Stern did receive another call from the draftboard. When the doctor saw his crippled spine he threw his hands up. "I'm afraid there isn't very much we can do with you," he said. "You just stay in your school, and teach those kids something sensible." Stern said that he'd like nothing better, and went back to school.

But even though Walter's warning had not helped him any, Stern thought about it frequently. He tried to get to know this complex young fellow better. He did not succeed.

There was a little cottage on the bank of the river, belonging to an influential member of the town council who was a close friend of the *Standartenführer's*. Once Walter picked up a remark at the dinner table about a "black pig" which this man kept. Walter concluded that a "black pig" must be a pig that hadn't been reported to the food ministry, and decided to take an interest in the beast.

For two days he explored the area around the cottage till he had gathered all the information he needed. Then he and Scholten—who else but he?—dragged his collapsible boat up the river and put it together some hundred feet away from the cottage. He put a canvas in the boat, set the boat in the water, and tied it to a rock on the bank.

They waited till the people who lived in the cottage went out, and approached the grounds, going up to the little outhouse where they suspected the pig was kept. Forst took his father's .38 pistol from the piece of linen in which he had wrapped it, and with two shots killed the animal. They dragged it across the gravelly soil to the river, and sweating, lifted the heavy load into the boat. Forst sat in the rear of the boat, and let his feet dangle out into the water on either side. He paddled downstream to the town, while Scholten covered the tracks behind them and went off through the bushes.

A nice juicy piece of meat, Forst thought, as he paddled lazily along. Dusk had already fallen when he reached town. A little further below, Scholten, Mutz, and Horber were waiting in a thicket. Horber expertly sawed the pig in half and carved it up. They each dragged home a share.

Mutz alone felt uneasy.

"Don't worry about it," Forst reassured him. "If he reports the theft, they'll ask him how come anyone can steal a pig he never owned in the first place. It was never reported, you see."

Next day at lunch the *Standartenführer* told them of the mean trick that had been played on his friend. They'd stolen a pig right from under his nose, and it wasn't even ready for slaughter. He was very upset because he had been looking forward to getting some of the delicacy.

"We're having pork for the next few days," Walter said dryly.

When he received no reply, he added: "By the way, there are two rounds missing in your pistol. I just tried it out yesterday!"

The *Standartenführer* had at last caught on. He gave his son a look of hate, but he said nothing. Not a word. And he enjoyed the pork during the next few days.

Walter Forst got his draft notice a day earlier than the others. He sat up alone that evening. His mother had gone to bed early—she had been feeling weaker of late. The *Standartenführer* was away traveling.

Walter went to the cellar and got a bottle of wine. Then he stole a pack of good, Egyptian pre-war cigarettes from his father's desk, put some of his Swiss jazz recordings on and stretched out in an easy chair. He smoked, drank, and listened to the music.

He was feeling great after the first bottle. That was when he threw his half-filled glass at the picture of the Führer on the wall because he thought for a moment that it was his father. The glass in front of the picture cracked into ugly long splinters. Under the picture there was a red spot on the wall.

Looks like blood, Walter Forst thought, and laughed.

Then he called for the maid and told her to clean the

broken glass away. He observed closely how high her skirt lifted as she bent over. Then he went to the cellar for a second bottle.

He put a new record on, listened enraptured to the fast rhythms and beat time to them with his foot. Funny, he thought, how a little alcohol can make life so much easier.

In a sudden fit of rage he went about the room smashing pictures, sweeping ashtrays and vases to the floor. In between he sat down and laughed out loud.

When he became aware of the mess he had made, he called again for the maid and said: "Come on, clean this up!"

When she had finished and wanted to walk out the door past him, he stood up and blocked her way. His legs were unsteady. "Now for the climax," he said, and grabbed her roughly. Afterwards she reproached him: "Your father is gentler!"

He had to go to the bathroom in the worst way, but couldn't quite make it and vomited in the hall.

Then he went to take a cold shower. What a pig I am, he thought. What an awful pig. Then he went to his mother's room and knelt at her bedside, pressed his face against her arm, and told her everything.

Dear God, she thought, what have I given birth to, what kind of son do I have?

And then she thought: Only you, God, know the pains he gave me when he was born. But he causes me more pain now than ever before!

Why can't he be still, she thought, why must he tell me all this?

And when Walter told her in a faint voice how he had

enjoyed beating up the man that time, his mother prayed: "Dear Lord, have mercy on him!"

*

All Scholten and Mutz could see below the arch after the smoke had cleared away was a crater on the gravelly bank, which was some six feet deep and was slowly filling with water. On one of the bridge-beams they saw a piece of Walter's jacket, and twenty yards further away the steel helmet full of blood.

Silently the two friends left the place. When they reached the bridge above, Albert Mutz put his arm around the shoulders of Ernst Scholten, and together they walked across to the eastern bank.

17

Silently, they walked side by side. From time to time Scholten and Mutz staggered as though they were about to lose their balance, and it made them aware of how tired they were.

Dead tired.

"We ought to walk faster," Mutz said. "The Amis could be here any moment!"

"Who cares?" Scholten replied. "I don't give a shit any more!"

He stopped in the middle of the bridge and looked at Albert Mutz with dull empty eyes.

"Tell me, Albert, that's you, isn't it? We did go to school together, didn't we? Slap my face, Albert, or kick me, or do anything I can feel. Else I'll think that I'm dreaming. Or gone mad. Am I mad? All this isn't true? I can't believe any of it!"

Scholten was almost screaming.

"It can't be true, Albert! There were seven of us only last night!"

And then Scholten sang. He shouted out, he bellowed:

Today Germany belongs to us . . .
Germany . . . Germany . . .
and tomorrow the whole world!

And in a lower voice: "We must go home to them, Albert. We must tell them . . . the mothers . . . and the fathers. The whole world . . . !"

Then the somber Scholten groaned, and weeping woefully, like a little child, he leaned against his friend's shoulder.

Albert's heart was aching. He couldn't explain to himself why he walked quietly beside his friend, supported him, listened to his outburst, instead of doing something foolishly insane.

He only said: "Don't ask me, Ernst. I can't think now. I know nothing now. I wouldn't know the simplest thing now. I only know that I want to sleep. Sleep a long time. I am that tired."

They had reached the eastern bank.

Scholten took his arm off Mutz's shoulders. He stopped, but Mutz did not let him loose.

"Come on," he said. "Come home with me!"

"Home?" Scholten asked, and stared straight ahead. Then he said: "Ah yes, of course, home!"

And then they both heard the truck.

"He's heading our way," Scholten said. "Maybe the General is sending men to relieve us?"

They stood rooted to the spot, and waited for the truck which was coming down towards them. The truck pulled up directly beside the two, and halted.

Lieutenant Hampel climbed out of the cab, and six men jumped off the rear of the truck. Hampel hailed the two pale, hollow-cheeked, dirt-splashed figures who were staring at him with expectation and an alarming cheerfulness.

"Come, come, get going," he called to his men. "You'll have to make it snappy. I don't want to get a bullet through my back, now that it's almost time to leave!"

Then he turned to the boys: "Well now, how goes it, you tired warriors! You've done yourselves proud! The General sends his compliments. Quite a stunt you pulled off here. Two tanks! Christ, that's really going strong. Well, boys, you can go home now."

The Lieutenant had more praise ready, but something about the faces disturbed him, as did the comical posture—half stooped, half sloppy—of the two figures before him. Still, they'd held out bravely, they deserve credit for that, he thought. And they are still young, not sufficiently drilled. They still have a lot to learn . . .

Only, not from me any more, Hampel thought further—not from me any more!

It occurred to him that he ought to say something more, but what? Then he had it, of course.

"The General's compliment is worth something, boys. That's only rarely given. You must tell that to your comrades too, you understand?"

And Scholten, the same Scholten who only minutes earlier had hung dejectedly to his friend's arm was now wide awake.

"Wouldn't you like to tell that to our comrades yourself?" he asked with a cutting voice.

The Lieutenant thought: Here is someone trying to get my goat, there is something wrong. But he didn't know what it was all about. He could tell from the sound of the voice: This one's irritable, belligerent. Close to the borderline of insubordination. He knew the type from the drill square: You've got to watch out for them. Best thing is to break their resistance ruthlessly, at once.

Then the Lieutenant thought that it would all be over soon anyway. That he and the boys might wind up in the same prison camp. And he remained friendly. Friendly, but emphatic.

"The General's compliment is meant for each and every one of you. All of you together have accomplished a remarkable feat. The praise is meant for each of you. Is that clear?"

"They'll be delighted," Scholten said. "They'll be simply delighted!"

Then he threw his arm out wide with so sudden a movement that the Lieutenant stepped back, nonplussed. "There they are, *Herr Leutnant,* waiting—for the General's compliments!"

The dark eyes in the boyish face were aglow, were burning with hatred.

He's gone mad, Albert Mutz thought. He's absolutely mad!

"We'd like to go home now, *Herr Leutnant,*" he said. "We're tired."

"You can knock off," the Lieutenant said graciously. Mutz saluted, grabbed Scholten's arm and dragged him along.

For about thirty feet he let himself be led along willingly. Suddenly he asked: "What are those bastards doing to our bridge, Albert? Can you see what they're doing?"

Albert Mutz said: "They've unloaded cases. They're opening the covers to the steel shafts now and stowing the cases inside them."

They walked on for another few feet, tired and silent. Then Scholten again: "Did you say cases?"

He stopped and took the sleeve of Mutz's rain-drenched jacket in his fist: "Cases? Do you know what that means?"

Mutz stared into his friend's feverish eyes. He's mad, he thought again.

"They'll blow the bridge up," he said, and at the same time felt a profound pain inside: They'll destroy the bridge, just like that . . . Why did we have to defend it then? Five are lying over there who've fought for this bridge!

When Mutz again looked into Ernst Scholten's eyes, he began to understand his friend.

"Never," Scholten said. Determinedly, he had forced this "never" through clenched teeth. "They won't destroy our bridge. I swear it to you—they won't."

"Our bridge," he said, Mutz thought, our bridge! And he thought further: He's right, isn't he? Isn't it in truth our bridge?

But Mutz felt no passion as he thought it, and he stood troubled before this Scholten who trembled with excitement, whose eyes were burning with rage.

Abruptly Scholten turned around, and walked back to the bridge. Mutz, who ran after him, saw Scholten take the sten gun off his shoulder, saw him stop for a moment while he examined the magazine and put it back in place.

Scholten heard the steps behind him. He knew that his friend wanted to stop him, and would do so if he caught up with him. He started to run. Some fifteen feet away from Lieutenant Hampel, he stopped.

"Leave the bridge intact!" he said softly, and Hampel thought again: He's dangerous, this boy is absolutely dangerous. He turned around and went over to his men at the shaft.

There were only four cases left outside. One man sat in the shaft and took them one after another, as they were handed to him. Two men were on the other side of the bridge, unloading the remaining cases from the truck alongside the opposite shaft.

Scholten followed the Lieutenant. Mutz had meanwhile caught up with his friend, and was tugging at his sleeve, trying to hold him, but Scholten merely turned his face around and looked at Mutz for a second. Then Mutz let go. "All right, Ernst," he said hoarsely. "You know that we're pals!"

Scholten stood before Hampel.

"You're not going to blow up the bridge," he said. He had his rifle at his hip, the finger of the right hand on the trigger.

"Don't be absurd," the Lieutenant said entreatingly, and there was fear in his eyes. His right hand was groping along his belt, towards the holster.

"Hands off," Scholten said threateningly. "And get off the bridge! Nothing's going to happen, if you scram now!"

The men at the shaft had stopped working, and waited in silence.

Hampel turned towards them. "Nobody said anything about quitting! Finish up here, and let's get it over with!"

His voice broke: "This isn't a kindergarten here. There's still a war on!"

The Lieutenant looked at his watch and thought: Damn it all, we should be gone by now. He screamed again: "Step on it, ram those things down and put the fuses to it. Two fuses to a shaft. And then let's be off!"

One of the men reached again for a case.

"Hands off," Scholten said, and looked at the man. At

that moment the Lieutenant got his pistol out and with his left hand loaded it. But he was no longer able to pull the trigger.

He was struck down by a bullet from a German army carbine, fired from a distance of about thirty feet.

And Albert Mutz stood there deadly pale, and put his rifle down.

ALBERT MUTZ AND THE FIFTH COMMANDMENT

"Thou shalt not kill," was the commandment Albert Mutz felt certain he'd never be tempted to break. A colored reproduction in the Old Testament his mother kept on her bookshelf showed how wroth the Lord was with Cain after he had slain Abel. Every time little Albert looked at this picture he shuddered before the anger that blazed in God's eyes. And he believed that he would never in his life be able to kill.

But once, when he was six years old, he would have choked his little black kitten if his mother hadn't stopped him in time. He had been holding the little creature on his lap, and suddenly it wanted to get away from him. Albert didn't let go; the kitten's sharp claws scratched him across his wrists. In the first pain he let go, but then rushed after the kitten, grabbed him with both hands and, blind with rage and pain, tried to choke him.

His mother slapped him without saying anything, and left him. He stood there, tears running down his cheeks. Then he felt the cat brushing against his legs, purring. In a sudden welling up of emotion he lifted the little black animal to him, and pressed his wet face against the soft fur, wishing to undo it all.

His mother watched him, smiling softly to herself.

At supper, when she handed him his plate of vegetables, she said: "By the way, Albert, I gave your sausage to the cat. That's all right with you, isn't it?"

He swallowed and nodded bravely, although he had been looking forward to sausage.

As he lay down to sleep that night, he prayed: "Dear God, please forgive me for having tortured my cat, and don't let him be angry with me any longer." And God showed Albert that he had heard his prayer. When his mother came into the room with the holy water for Albert, the cat stole into the room after her. With one leap he was on Albert's bed and lay down on his shoulder, pressing his velvety fur against the boy's cheek. Then he began to purr. Happily, Albert Mutz fell asleep. His mother had to laugh when she turned the light off and left the room.

But Albert Mutz had learned that day only that one must not hurt a cat. A few days later a friend came visiting, and together they looked at his mother's photographs. It was difficult to determine afterwards how the argument between them had started. They both probably wanted to look at the same album at the same time. It ended with Albert's grabbing hold of the heavy book, and throwing it full force at his friend's stomach. The friend screeched and howled as if he were being roasted alive. Albert's mother used the feather duster she happened to have in her hand at the time on her son.

The following day they went to church together. His mother stopped before a painting that portrayed in crude and drastic fashion the tortures of the condemned souls in purgatory. Albert stared long at the gruesome picture before which a few candles were burning. Then he asked: "What are they doing, *Mami?*" Asked it in his thin, high voice so that his mother was barely able to repress a smile.

"They atone for their sins, Albert," she said.

"What's that, atone?"

"If anyone does evil, Albert, it hurts God very much. Because God, who has created the whole world and you and me, loves us all. And he doesn't want people to hurt each other, it makes him sad. To do evil is to commit a sin, and one must atone for sins. Must repent. That's why people who do evil are afraid. It is called having a guilty conscience!"

"I don't ever want to do evil," Albert promised. "Let's go, please?" And they left.

Two years had passed when Albert received for his birthday the little air rifle he had long been wishing for. His aunt gave it to him; his mother was by no means pleased with the gift.

Albert built a shooting gallery in the hall of his apartment. The hall was some twenty feet long. His mother hung a heavy felt mat on the door, and they fastened the target on it.

Albert Mutz stood there, shooting away. His friend stood next to him and waited to get a chance at it once. For about half an hour he waited patiently, then he said: "Please, Albert, let me once!"

But Albert wanted to try another three rounds. Only three. And after he had fired those three he wanted three more. This went on until his friend finally tired of waiting, and took hold of Albert's rifle at the barrel. Albert held on to the butt end, and they both pulled and quarreled loudly. Suddenly Mutz yanked the rifle from the other boy's hand with a violent pull. Screaming, his friend let go. The sight on the barrel had made a deep cut in the palm of his hand.

'The boy screamed and gaped at his hand, from which blood was dripping profusely onto the light wooden floor.

Albert stood frozen. He was frightened; he had a guilty conscience. After his mother had bandaged the boy's hand and taken him to the doctor, she spanked her son soundly.

It always cost her an effort to hit the boy. Sometimes he'd interrupt her, and say in his high voice: "Enough, *Mami!*"

Then she always had to leave the room quickly.

She believed that the physical punishment was necessary. When Albert wanted to have the rifle again in the afternoon, his mother told him: "I gave it to your friend, Albert. It gave him so much pain, he should have it now. Don't you think so?"

And again he swallowed his tears, and nodded bravely.

They didn't live in particularly comfortable circumstances. With the modest sum she received monthly she not only had to take care of the house, dress the youngsters and pay for their school books, but had to pay off debts as well. The debts of her husband. She never liked to talk about this subject.

The man who had promised her the moon some years earlier walked out on her one day. He left her with two boys and a vast number of creditors. Albert was still a baby at the time, less than a year old. Somehow Frau Mutz was able to manage. Her charm, her tenacity, and above all the awareness that the two boys needed her had helped. The day Albert Mutz celebrated his tenth birthday was a memorable day for her. The radio had announced that German troops had marched into Poland to safeguard certain interests, and Konrad Mutz told his mother that he had volunteered for the air force officers' training school. On this day too, the last of the creditors declared that he was satisfied with the sum received and would waive the balance. And he also told Frau Monika Mutz of his desire to marry her, if she on her part were well disposed to such an offer.

That was a bit too much all at once. On the evening of this hot September day she sat by the open window of her apartment and wondered whether it had been a good day or a bad one. It had been a good day for her, but the fear of war, fear for her oldest son, overshadowed all. Deeply moved, she watched Albert playing on the floor with his tin soldiers. He at least is not going to leave, she thought. He'll remain here with me.

Later she wrote to her husband's last creditor. She thanked him for his noble gesture, and showed between the lines how much joy his offer had given her. And yet, she wrote, the only task she saw before her now lay in the bringing up of her two sons. And though she couldn't accept his offer of marriage, she hoped he would remain a dear friend always.

As she sat before the mirror and combed her long blond hair, Albert came in to say good night. He looked up at her admiringly: "You're beautiful, *Mami*," he said with conviction. She had to laugh because his voice gave no indication of becoming more grown-up. After Albert left, Monika Mutz knew that his statement had been the nicest she had heard all day.

Fourteen days later Konrad Mutz went into the service. At first he wrote long letters. Then the letters became shorter, and more and more frequently he wrote things like: "If you can possibly get hold of a hard salami, or a cake that won't spoil . . ." Or: "Some guys here trade their meat rations for cigarettes."

Konrad, as well as Albert, was used to sitting down to a full table. They never knew abundance or prosperity, but neither did they ever want. They had never gone to bed hungry. They had often worn patched shirts and trousers and stockings, but never torn ones. Long after they had gone to bed, their mother sat at the sewing machine, patching, mending, and making things for them till late into the night. What she had accomplished and was still accomplishing, her sons could hardly begin to know.

One day Albert Mutz walked proudly into the house and held a five-mark bill under his mother's nose. "Here, this is for you."

He was taken aback by his mother's reaction. She wasn't at all pleased. On the contrary; she seemed rather upset. He was perplexed by the sharpness of her question. "Where did you get the money, Albert?"

"I went to pick berries with my friends," he said defensively. "We put them in paper bags and sold them. Thirty pennies a bag. Then we divided the money. Is that bad?"

No, it was not bad. Only his mother didn't want it. She didn't want him to have money in his pockets, she didn't want him to have anything to do with money at all. Let him come to her if he needed anything.

But how was she to explain that to him? How was she to make him understand her fear that he might turn out like his father? Was she to punish him because he had picked berries and had sold them, when the other boys had done the same? No, since he knew nothing of his father's story, he couldn't possibly understand. Some day he'd learn about it.

"Listen, Albert," she said. "I'm not sure you'll understand this. But you know we have our pride. Wouldn't it be embarrassing if you approached some woman with your berries, and she'd talk about it to other people: 'Things must be bad for the Mutzes. They're even sending the little one out peddling berries, in order to make ends meet!' "

Albert looked at his mother, expecting more, but when he saw that she had finished, he replied: "We can't afford that, Mommy, of course not. I'll tell my friends and we'll split up in two groups. One to do the picking, and another to do the selling. I'll just pick, and no one will know about it."

His mother realized then that her little boy could be nice and sweet, not just temperamental and given to sudden fits of rage, and that he also had inherited that cunning intelligence of his father's that the creditors still talked about.

"Dear God," she prayed that evening, "let it at least be a healthy combination, and I'll be content."

Albert Mutz could be stingy, but he could also be extravagantly generous. He could on the spur of the moment give his lunch to a poor boy who had none and who stood in the school yard hungrily staring at the sandwiches of other children. Like a prince he'd walk over to the boy and in passing press his lunch bag into his hand: "Here, take it."

But he expected the same generosity from others.

Once a friend of his received a ten-mark bill. Albert had never seen so much money before. He immediately had an idea. Why not buy toys with it, and so as not to lose any time, right after school. They went to a toy store. Albert Mutz picked a beautiful tank, one that spit fire from two barrels when in motion and climbed easily over hurdles. To the boy with the money he generously recommended the purchase of a little steamboat. Interestedly, he watched the money disappear in the cash register, clutched the tank under his arm and went home. It was only when he saw his mother that he began to have misgivings. He wondered if she'd approve of the deal.

She did not approve, and spanked him until he told her that he had finally understood the difference between "mine" and "thine." Then she sent him back to the store to return the tank, and sent the money to the boy's parents. Albert had never before seen his mother so angry.

He decided to avoid shopping in the future. He became, in fact, afraid of money. Instead of buying something for Mother's Day, he composed a poem for his mother. He was pressed for time and couldn't finish the last verse. He took one of the red books from the bookcase, and copied some lines. When he reread them, he became dissatisfied with his own verses.

He threw the whole thing away, and started over again, but this time he copied the entire poem from the red book. It sounded fine when he read the poem to himself half aloud.

His mother was genuinely pleased, but couldn't help laughing, although Albert had been under the impression that it was rather a solemn poem. She asked him: "Did you write it all by yourself?"

He nodded, beaming with pride: "I did. I copied it all by myself—from the red book, you know?"

She knew. Her ten-year-old son had dedicated to her for Mother's Day the poem "Ganymed" by Johann Wolfgang von Goethe, no less.

Until he reached the age of fourteen, Albert had to give a strict accounting to his mother of where he spent the afternoons. Evenings he had to be home. She was less strict later, but she still wanted to know where he spent his time.

Most of the time he was home anyway, up in the big garret. It was his favorite hideout.

Much as other boys loved to play with electric trains, he was attached to his toy soldiers. He never did more for school than was absolutely essential. He rushed through his homework, then stormed up the stairs to the garret and was not to be seen again for hours. No matter how few his mother's Christmas presents to him were, there were always some toy soldiers. His aunts—Albert had five—knew his hobby and never let him down.

With old shoe boxes, linen and wrapping paper, he had constructed a veritable town up in the garret. An endless column of marching men moved through its streets, led off by a military band. Outside the town lay the strategic hill from which the General Staff surveyed the battlefield. His mother had spent the nights of Christmas putting the battlefield together. It had trenches, *chevaux-de-frise,* a few bunkers, and an undulating terrain. Toy soldiers in German, British and French uniforms stood facing each other. There was even one Moroccan in a white burnous among them, brandishing a rifle. Infantrymen in field-gray uniforms and hussars with glittering swords fought side by side. He had a first-aid station complete with ambulances and stretchers, an anti-aircraft site with searchlights, cannons, and a few heavy tanks. The cannons were loaded with rubber stoppers and percussion caps and had a range of some six feet.

Off to one side was a blockhouse, manned by cowboys. Around it was a swarm of hostile Indians. Still more Indians danced around a stake to which was tied a paleface, desperately hoping for deliverance. All of that was to be found in Albert's garret, and it was there that he fought his battles.

If he had two or three friends with him, his enthusiasm knew no bounds. There was only one rule to the game: Albert Mutz's army had to win, no matter if on a given day he happened to command Germans, Frenchmen, cowboys or Indians. It was a rule to which his friends tacitly agreed.

Little Albert Mutz fired his men with rousing speeches before letting them advance into the main lines of the battle. When distributing the weapons, and especially the cannons, he made sure to keep the best for himself. That there was a connection between the battles he waged in the attic and the war raging in the world outside never entered his mind.

Wednesday afternoons he went to the Hitler Youth meetings in the clubhouse or in the arena. He rather liked going. Most of the time they sang, and every now and then they marched into the woods for scouting games that were only a variation on the familiar cowboys and Indians.

Once a soldier in field-gray uniform came to talk to the boys about the war and about the heroism of German soldiers. At the end of his talk he asked how many of them wanted to become officers. They all did, with the exception of Albert Mutz.

"What is it you want to be, lad?"

"I want to be an engineer on a locomotive!" Albert had just come back the day before from a train trip.

"But Germany needs soldiers, why don't you want to be a soldier?"

Mutz stubbornly: "Because I'd rather be an engineer!"

At this point his troopleader cut in. "He wants to be an engineer because he is a shithead!" he said amidst general laughter.

Albert Mutz wasn't used to being called names, especially in public. Tears came to his eyes. "I'm not a shithead," he shouted, took his uniform cap and walked out.

The troopleader screamed after him to stay, but Mutz walked right down the hall, down the stairs of the huge building, and out the door. Next day the troopleader met Albert's mother on the street, and ignored her completely. She mentioned it at home in passing. The next time Albert saw the troopleader he brushed hard by him and stared into the troopleader's face, but made no attempt to salute. The troopleader took him to task for it, called him a stubborn ass whom they'd know how to bring to heel. Mutz replied in a low voice but with firmness that he had no reason to salute the troopleader as long as the troopleader ignored his mother.

A day later Albert was informed in writing that because of insubordination he was no longer permitted to wear the uniform. The same mail also brought a letter from his brother. He had received a high decoration. His mother took the letter to the party headquarters. "Listen," she said to the troopleader. "I won't have a shirker like you bully my boy, while my other son is out there, daily risking his life!" She left him without waiting for an answer. Nothing happened for a while.

In the course of one of the subsequent classes *Studienrat* Stern casually dropped a remark to the effect that Germany also needed engineers. Sometimes they're even more important than soldiers. "Quite so!" Walter Forst chimed in, and laughed.

Stern had turned red in the face. "It wasn't meant that way, Forst," he said softly. Mutz was overjoyed. He didn't know that two days later a man in civvies called on Stern to ask him what his remark was supposed to mean.

"Just what it said," Stern replied dryly.

Did he by any chance doubt the favorable outcome of the war? To this Stern replied that he had no doubts whatsoever about the outcome of the war. With this the interrogation was ended. But Stern brooded about who in the class had snitched on him. It was Albert himself. He told everyone he met that his teacher had agreed with him.

A week later the school board came. It was Mutz's turn to proclaim the weekly motto. Stern was teaching the first hour that morning. At eight o'clock sharp he walked into the classroom together with the school board. The board consisted of three elderly gentlemen, two of them civilians and one in uniform. The class saluted, and then Mutz blared the motto for the week into the room:

"The youth of Germany is the guardian of the future!"

That went well. But almost immediately another voice added: "In a common grave!"

Quiet.

Studienrat Stern had become red in the face. The three men looked at him, perplexed. "Strange," one of them said at last. "Very strange, don't you agree, *Herr Kollege?*" And he again regarded *Studienrat* Stern, who was desperately seeking for a way out.

"Forst," he said. "What did you mean by this stupid remark?" Walter stood up slowly, feeling suddenly quite uncomfortable too. He had after all only intended his remark for Ernst Scholten, who sat in front of him, not for the commission. He had to find something that would take the matter out of politics, but what? He had an idea.

"Herr Professor, I merely said it because I don't like Mutz, and wanted it to appear that he had said it."

Mutz turned around for a split second and winked at Forst. Thank God he understood, Forst thought, he has caught on. After that they piled it on even thicker. Mutz confirmed that he and Forst didn't get along, and *Studienrat* Stern turned to the commission and said: "It's frightful . . . these two. The best students, but they are always competing. Always accusing each other, hurting each other."

"Very strange," the man from the school board said once again. "This sort of thing does not reflect well on the school." Then he turned to Forst: "What does your father do, my boy?"

"My father is *Standartenführer,*" Forst said in a friendly tone. The man from the school board turned to Stern, suddenly comprehending. Stern shrugged his shoulders, as if to confirm that of course he was helpless under the circumstances. The commission did get a better impression of the class in the course of the period. After the three gentlemen left, Stern walked over to Forst's bench with quick, short steps, and slapped Walter Forst in the face. "Jackass!" he said. "You and your big mouth are going to get the whole class into trouble!" It was the first time that Stern had ever hit a student. And Forst, who wouldn't let anyone touch him, merely nodded his head as though to say: "I had that coming."

One fine day Konrad Mutz came home on furlough. Albert was so pleased to be walking next to the young man in his Lieutenant's uniform that Konrad had not the heart to put on civvies. Albert blushed each time a soldier smartly saluted his big brother. After a while he got used to it and began watching like a hawk for anyone who failed to do so. "Did you see that?" he'd say, nudging his brother. "He didn't salute us."

Konrad laughed.

At home, when talking to his mother, Konrad never laughed. They always talked so low that Albert could hardly understand a word of what they said.

Lieutenant Mutz left again one day and Albert that very evening ran up to the attic he had neglected for so long. What he saw was a scene of destruction. All his toy soldiers trampled on and crumbled to dust, his guns bent. The work of some madman who with heavy boots had laid waste the carefully arranged little town.

Crying, Albert ran to his mother, and she came to inspect the damage. "What a silly boy," she said. "As if his doing this will change anything." But Albert never got out of her whom she had meant.

It would have taken him a long time to get over this if it hadn't been for a girl who had just come into his class. She was as tall as he, had dark blond hair, and he liked her from the first moment on. With his mother's consent, he asked the "new one" to his birthday party. Albert was fourteen at the time. The girl's name was Traudl and she came from a wealthy and respected family that had an estate not far from the town. Her parents had sent her there when the air raids in the big city became more and more frequent. With a grandmother and an old aunt she now lived in the big villa.

Enthusiastically, Albert accepted her invitation two days later to visit her there. The enormous park in the midst of which the grand house was situated, the little swimming pool, the well-tended lawn and the big chicken house all impressed him equally. They played nicely to-

187

gether half of the afternoon, throwing a big rubber ball
to each other. Seeing Traudl romping about in her white
linen suit made him think again of how well he liked
her.

Once the ball fell into the pool, and while Albert was
still looking for a pole to fish it out she jumped laughing
and giggling into the water, swam up to it and threw it
out onto the lawn. Then she climbed out of the pool, her
linen suit clinging to her body and transparent.

Albert Mutz stared at the girl, and then laughed out
loud. "Hahaha," he burst out. "How funny you look!"

He nearly choked laughing.

Traudl looked down at herself, then ran into the
house. She stopped before the large mirror in the hall.
Upset and red with shame, she looked at herself in the
mirror, and then ran up the stairs to her room, threw herself on the bed and wept. Albert meanwhile waited
patiently beside the pool. Tired of waiting at last, he
went into the house to look for her. She was just coming
down the stairway, wearing a bright summer dress.

On the landing she stopped and looked down at him.
Highly insulted. "You're a stupid fool," she said. "I want
you to go home now."

Startled and embarrassed, Albert looked at her. Suddenly he became aware of what she had said. She had
thrown him out. He left the house, blushing with shame
and fury, and stepped so hard on the pedal of his bicycle
that the chain snapped. Now on top of everything he
even had to walk home.

In the evening Traudl told the story to her aunt when
she asked why the nice boy hadn't stayed for coffee. Her
aunt listened attentively and then said, smiling: "Albert
Mutz is a nice dear boy, really quite different from most.

If I were you, I'd give this another thought. I personally prefer boys who laugh at such times than the other kind."

Albert too told the story to his mother and interrupted her indignantly: "But you're also laughing!"

"Of course, Albert," she said. "I can well understand why you laughed."

But she thought it only right to tell the boy why the girl felt insulted by his laughter. Nor did she stop there, but went on explaining why nature had created two different sexes. Albert Mutz was proud that his mother talked to him as to a grown-up, but it wasn't all quite clear to him yet.

"You'll understand it some day," his mother said. "Everyone does. Only if you have any more questions, I want you to come to me and ask."

He promised that he would.

Walter Forst once asserted: "Mutz definitely has a retarded ignition!" For a while Albert regarded this criticism as a decided flaw in himself. Then he forgot about it again. They once had to translate a long Latin sentence in class. The sentence told of boys and girls long ago bathing together entirely nude in the lakes and streams, with only those participating who were still untouched. Mutz promptly raised his hand, and asked the teacher: "Why, *Fräulein Doktor?*"

A few in the class laughed out loud. Mutz turned red, and the teacher told him he'd have to stay in after class that afternoon. Just the afternoon on which he was going to be out playing with his friends. Furiously, he told the story to his mother at lunch time, and she tried to explain it to him.

"Go to the principal, please," he said. "Have him revoke the punishment!" But his mother declined emphatically. "An hour after class won't do you any harm in any case."

It turned out rather nicely at that. The Latin instructress had brought a pile of copybooks to correct, and she gave him a short exercise to translate. He sat there sweating over it, and once looked to the desk where the teacher sat. The rays of the afternoon sun touched her dark hair with a silver sheen, and as she sat there, so serious and self-contained, bending over her copybooks, she suddenly seemed quite attractive to Albert.

He said softly: *"Fräulein Doktor!"*

She hadn't heard him, and he repeated a little louder: *"Fräulein Doktor!"*

She looked up now. "I want to apologize for this morning. I . . ." He hesitated. "I really meant the question seriously. I'm sorry I am so dumb. My mother meanwhile explained it all!"

She got up and walked over to him, and sat down on his school bench.

"I'm sorry, Albert, but when the class laughed I had to assume it was pre-arranged. I'm really sorry now. You aren't angry with me, are you?"

He blushed again; no teacher had ever talked that way to him.

"Not at all," he said, embarrassed.

"Well, run along home now and give your mother my best. I'll still drop her a few lines." Smiling, she watched him run out of the classroom.

His mother got two letters in the morning mail. One informed her that Konrad had been taken a prisoner by the British. The second letter was from the Latin teacher and told her that she could be proud of little Albert.

Both letters pleased her very much. Konrad was safe. He had come through it all right. Before he left to return to the front he had told her: "Mother, I'm afraid. I may not come through it alive!"

"Trust in Him, Konrad," she had replied, pointing to the little black crucifix over the door.

The summer after this, Albert begged his mother to let him go on a trip with Scholten—to the large lake in the South. They'd take their bikes, would sleep out in tents, and they'd be ever so good—really, really. His mother spent sleepless nights before she agreed to let him go.

The big day came at last. The summer holidays started. They were to be the most beautiful holidays. With tents, with an enormous rucksack and with a whole litany of good advice, Albert Mutz and Ernst Scholten set out. They parked the bikes near the lake and rented a canoe for a ridiculously paltry sum. Happily they rowed over to the uninhabited little island whose rocks sloped gently down into the lake.

They pitched their tents and cooked their first tea on a little kerosene burner. Ernst Scholten took out his flute and played. In the morning they crept out of the tent in their sweat suits, undressed and jumped into the icy water. Then they had breakfast and afterwards lay in the sun side by side.

Simple but unforgettable days these were for both of them. They didn't talk much, never quarreled. They were either in the water or roaming about on the island.

One afternoon they had fallen asleep on the rocks when Mutz suddenly woke up. Scholten was gone. He looked for the canoe and saw that it too was missing. Reassured, he wanted to lie down again at first, but he jumped up anyway and looked out to the lake. There wasn't a boat in sight. The lake was turbulent and there were white crests on the waves.

A nameless terror suddenly gripped Mutz. Something must have happened to Ernst, he thought. Something certainly happened to him or I'd see him. He ran down the length of the island and looked out to all sides without seeing his friend.

He wept. Ernst drowned, what am I to do, he surely drowned! The lake seemed no longer friendly and kind, the waves were threatening and the wind blew cold. Mutz prayed.

"Dear God, please let nothing have happened to Ernst," he prayed. "I promise you I'll go into a monastery, if nothing happened to him!"

At that very moment he saw the boat, a tiny speck far off and the oars moving. You beast, Mutz thought. You're having a gay old time rowing around, and I'll have to go into a monastery now. He was beginning to have pangs of conscience about the affair.

When Scholten brought the boat in and climbed out, Mutz told him that he had promised to become a monk for his sake. Mutz had too much sun, Scholten thought, I'll have to handle him carefully.

"Whom did you promise that?" he asked piously. Indignantly, Mutz answered: "Whom, whom? God, of course!"

Scholten whistled through his teeth, he could do that. This is serious, he thought, and said aloud: "You don't really know though if God wants you to become a monk?"

"No," Mutz replied, annoyed. "But a promise is a promise, that much is certain."

"Well," Scholten said. "You still have lots of time to reconsider calmly and quietly."

Alluding to the fact that the free life would soon come to an end for him, Scholten got his friend to go along the following morning for a look at the fishing nets. They found two trout in the first one they came across and carried them off. The day after, alluding once again to the imminent, severe, monkish life, Scholten induced Mutz to help him take three trout back to their little island.

On the fourth day the old constable came rowing over towards their island, sweating and cursing. When he came ashore, Scholten snapped to attention and saluted smartly.

Strapping lads, the old man thought, they wouldn't steal. Or would they?

"No," Scholten asserted boldly. "We happen not to like fish, as a matter of fact." He cast a sidelong glance to the willow twig, stuck between two rocks, from which hung suspended the four trout they had taken out of the nets that morning.

They offered to go out next morning to see if anyone was about the nets. "There are two of them," the constable said. "They've been seen."

He removed his cap and wiped his forehead with a big red handkerchief. They made him tea, and accompanied him a stretch in their own canoe.

"How about that," Scholten shouted for joy. "We have a free hand now to filch as much as we like. All quite legal too, in the service of the police!"

But Albert Mutz was fed up with it.

Even beautiful holidays must end, and Albert was home again one day. There was a letter from his aunt waiting for him. She asked him if he would like to help

193

with the harvest for two weeks. How he'd like that! The school had to give him two weeks off.

Two days later he traveled to his aunt's farm. He worked very hard there for two weeks. Two interesting weeks.

The majority of his aunt's workers were either French, Polish, or Yugoslav. The only German was an old servant of the house, close to seventy. Three German girls worked in the stable, together with one French girl and two Polish girls. They seemed to get on well. Food was plentiful and his aunt didn't drive anyone, partly because she was afraid of the foreign laborers.

Evenings they sat in the barn and sang. One man played the accordion, and there was dancing—polkas and waltzes. A bottle of whiskey would suddenly appear and be passed around. Then the men would raise their voices, laughing, shouting and sometimes even quarreling a little.

Albert was not to go to the barn. His aunt usually sat in the big kitchen behind the well-polished oak table and read the newspaper. On the bench beside her she kept a big pistol. The foreigners made her uneasy, partly because she couldn't understand their language.

But the German maids went over to the barn sometimes, and nothing ever happened to them. At least nothing they didn't want to have happen. Twice his aunt had called the constable in the middle of the night, and had asked him to come out and check up. He pedaled to the farm on his bicycle, went over to the barn and was received with a howling welcome. Somebody handed him the whiskey bottle, and he wasn't above taking a nip before he left again.

One evening Albert Mutz went over anyway. At first they took no notice of him, but then one of the men moved aside to make room for him and motioned to him to sit down. He listened to the accordion, hummed along, and enjoyed himself very much in this circle.

When the whiskey bottle made the rounds again, he wasn't overlooked. After the second or third sip the whiskey no longer burnt his throat as much as it had after the first. They watched him with amusement, and slapped his back when the liquid went down the wrong way.

Then they danced, whirling about in time to the music. They stamped on the rough planks of the barn, and suddenly stepped back to form a large circle. The accordion player stood up, opened his arms wide and played an exciting, fiery tune.

From somewhere a white figure flitted into the circle of men. It was the French girl who worked in the stable.

She stood there for a moment, barefoot, in a bright skirt, a flame-red blouse, her arms raised high.

Then she began to twirl around, and strands of her black hair fell over her forehead. Faster and faster she whirled. She stepped forward towards the circle of men, laughingly evaded a quick hand reaching out for her, showed her teeth like a wildcat, and stared about her with shiny eyes.

There was a break in the music. She reeled over to the nearest man and fell into his arms.

Once again the whiskey bottles were passed, men sang, the accordionist played and Frenchie stepped into the center of the circle once more. This time she sang, holding a cigarette in her hand. It was a melancholy song, the words of which Albert could not understand.

The pace of the music became faster again. The woman let her cigarette fall down and stepped on it with her bare foot; then danced again.

She turned so fast that her skirt flew up way over her

hips. With wide-open eyes and moist lips, the men stared at her naked legs, her smooth thighs. Albert felt the excitement in the atmosphere of the room and wanted to leave. In the door he stopped and turned around for a last look, taking in the scene: A woman dancing in a circle of lustful men.

Albert Mutz couldn't fall asleep that night. He now understood what his mother had meant when she had said: "You'll understand one day, everyone does!"

The picture that he had carried away from the barn both excited and repelled him. The faces of the men repelled him. He couldn't fall asleep. He got up, dressed, and rode out into the night on his bicycle.

When he came to the brook, he suddenly had an idea. He put the bike into the ditch, stripped bare, then plunged into the cold water. He dived under several times until he was blue in the face and his teeth chattered. The he came out and rode back to the farm.

He put the bike away and saw that the light was still on in the room where the maids slept. At that moment, the woman who had danced in the barn was pulling her slip over her head. She is beautiful, he thought. More beautiful than can be imagined. And then he thought: I could have done without that cold swim.

He was very tired by the time he was in bed again, and soon fell fast asleep.

He often passed the barn during the following evenings. But he didn't go in to join the men. Once he could not resist the temptation, and looked in. He wanted to see her dance. A few couples were dancing, but Frenchie sat on the lap of a burly blond man, drinking from a whiskey bottle. Albert Mutz dreamed that night that he had killed the blond man. He had to laugh when he remembered the dream in the morning.

The day before his departure they had a feast. The harvest was completed. His aunt thanked the workers and had an exceptionally good meal for them. Afterwards the accordionist played, Frenchie sang, and several bottles of whiskey were passed around. One of the men made a speech that Albert couldn't understand, and when he had finished he walked up to Albert's aunt and kissed her hand. Albert smiled when he saw his aunt, frightened, pull her hand away and hide it under the apron.

From the left they handed him a bottle, and he drank. Another bottle came from the right, and he drank again, God knows how many times. Somehow he found himself standing next to Frenchie in the middle of the circle of men. The men laughed and clapped their hands as she put her own hands on his hips and whirled him around, right and left, in time to the music. When the music stopped, she gave him a kiss and he beamed.

Albert Mutz staggered back to the house. He lay down on the bed with his clothes and shoes still on and fell asleep. The following morning he went home.

There were surprises in store for him at home. Traudl returned his hello again, and was as sweet and friendly as she had been before that incident by the pool. They went to the theater one evening.

A stock company was putting on *Iphigenia*. Traudl was absorbed in the performance, but Albert was a trifle bored. He kept looking sideways at his girl throughout, while up on the stage they were speaking all these valuable lines. After the play he took her home.

They bicycled side by side, and Albert thought that a bike can be a real nuisance at times. When they came to an incline, one that he usually rode up, he got off the bicycle, but she let him down. Bravely she struggled up the hill and waited for him till he caught up with her.

The girl has no feelings, he thought, but I'm going to kiss her!

They got off the bikes at the gate of the estate. The time had come. For a short moment he pressed his lips to hers, and she let it happen.

It had been ever so slight and fleeting, almost like a breath of air. And yet more.

Albert Mutz felt her full, soft lips and the taste of some cosmetic on his tongue when he passed it over his lips.

He thought: There was something wrong. It wasn't really a kiss. Traudl was already on the inside of the gate by the time he had come to the end of his deliberations, and she held out a small cool hand to him from within. He shook it mechanically and stared after her.

Suddenly he called her name. Traudl turned and came back down the gravel path to the gate. Mutz put his bike down and walked inside the garden towards her.

"I forgot something," he said and took her head between his hands, almost violently, and kissed her. It took considerably longer this time because he wouldn't let go. Traudl slapped him afterwards and said: "You're horrible!" And was off.

But it didn't sound very convincing, and Mutz rode home on his bike whistling happily. "My lodging's in the field, and on a rock I rest my weary bones!"

In an old illustrated weekly he came across an intriguing picture of a Midsummer Night festival attended by some Nazi big shots. Four girls represented a scene from Greek mythology, and were dressed accordingly. That is to say, they wore absolutely nothing. It was precisely what appealed to Mutz about the picture. He cut it out neatly and pasted it on a white cardboard, then hung it in his room.

"This isn't the picture for a boy's room," his mother said.

"Is it bad?" he asked with feigned innocence.

"No, but in poor taste," his mother replied.

This was a few days after his fifteenth birthday.

Traudl had increased her hold on Mutz to such an extent that he had no intentions of doing anything foolish. At the same time she knew how to hold him off and he had few illusions about any serious adventures with her. But once they came very close.

They had a date one evening, and bicycled together to the little lake near the town. They untied one of the boats and rowed out. The stars gleamed in the sky, the weather was still mild, and far and wide nothing stirred. They lay side by side in the boat. They pressed close to one another. But just as Mutz was about to swear eternal love to Traudl, the sirens went off.

Silently they rowed back, mounted their bikes, and rode home. Traudl stopped once along the way and said to Albert Mutz: "Don't be angry now, but I'm glad the sirens went off just then." Albert wasn't at all glad, but he feigned understanding.

Scholten came frequently to Mutz's house, and joined Albert's mother at the piano. Many afternoons the two of them were outdoors, in the woods and fields and on the nearby lakes. Once an American bomber was shot down nearby. While the search squads were still out hunting for it, Scholten and Mutz were already busy emptying the plane.

Aluminum plates, baskets of ammunition, cigarettes, chocolate, safety belts, a rubber dinghy, a pistol, and many more things were stored away in Mutz's cellar before the German soldiers found the plane. They saw them coming at last as they were just about to dismantle the machine gun. The two still managed to disappear in the last moment.

One Sunday Mutz went to the barracks for pre-military training. During history class the next day he told Scholten that there were open cases of carbines in the halls of the barracks. Scholten was immediately inspired.

"Let's get a pair!"

Mutz helped his friend over the wall of the barracks that evening, and waited for him outside.

It took a long time. I hope they haven't caught him, Mutz thought, when he heard the signal they had agreed on.

He climbed up the wall, took the two brand-new carbines Scholten handed him, and pulled his friend up to him on the wall. They slid down to the street and ran home through the forest with the carbines concealed in a piece of canvas.

Mutz put the rifles under his mattress. His mother found them there on Friday, when she did the thorough cleaning.

"Where did you get these?"

Albert, instead of giving a straight answer, said lightly: "Times are rather unquiet, Mother. We should have something in the house."

"Get them out of here," his mother said. He promised that he would.

They were still in the same place the following Friday, but since his mother was deadly afraid of all shooting weapons she let them lie there. And after a while they were forgotten.

On the afternoon when Mutz received the notice to appear in the barracks he rewrapped the rifles in the canvas and carried them into the nearby forest. He had discovered a hollow tree there a while back. He stuck the carbines into it, and ran home. Then he took the pistol that he had taken from the American plane and placed it under a bottom board in his room.

He took the picture of the four Graces—the one his mother had found in poor taste—and he burnt it.

It took him at least fifteen minutes to leaf through the pages of a diary he had started years ago, but had soon discarded again. Every now and then he read a page, was vastly amused, then threw the book into the fireplace. He burnt everything that he didn't think essential and worth preserving. Even Traudl's letters.

That done, he sat down to write the girl a few lines. Several times he tore the page and began anew. Everything he put down on paper seemed untrue, wordy, full of platitudes and pathos.

Then he simply wrote:

Dear Traudl, I've got to go in the Service now and probably won't see you for some time. I'll be true to you. Don't forget me.

Yours, Albert.

On rereading, he crossed out the "I'll be true to you," and rewrote the changed version. He put the letter in an envelope, addressed it, and took it down to the mail box. When he returned he found Ernst Scholten already waiting for him.

Albert Mutz had never bothered to think about his relationship to Ernst Scholten. He only began to think about it on the bridge, and when they trudged back after the Americans had withdrawn, Mutz thought: Funny, he's my best friend and he was spared.

Later still, when Scholten turned on the Lieutenant of the demolition squad, Mutz knew that he had come to a decisive point. Were he to decide on the basis of what he had learned in his history classes, then he'd have to turn against his friend, for then Scholten clearly was a mutineer, a saboteur, a traitor.

But Scholten was his friend.

Scholten had said "our bridge," and Mutz knew that he was right. On the other hand, Scholten wasn't being very logical. If they hadn't defended the bridge the Americans would have been across by now, and then Hampel would not find himself in the postition of having to blow it up.

Albert Mutz thought and found that there was no end to these considerations. He stood there, the carbine at his hip, and waited.

With paralyzing dread Mutz saw then that the Lieutenant was reaching for his pistol. Scholten had turned his back on the Lieutenant and didn't notice.

Mutz hesitated. He had seen the Lieutenant load the pistol. Now the Lieutenant pointed the pistol at Scholten's back. And in this instant Mutz's brooding came to an end. He no longer thought about his history classes, about treason and mutiny. He only saw Ernst Scholten standing there and behind him a man who was about to shoot his friend in the back.

Mutz yanked the carbine up to his shoulder, looked at the blurred figure of the Lieutenant through the gunsight and fired.

He fired again, placed the rifle at "safe" and lowered it to his hip again.

Dazed, he stared at the Lieutenant who was slumping forward and falling on his face. Albert Mutz heard his mother say: Thou shalt not kill, thou shalt harm neither man nor beast, thou shalt cause no pain to others. God wills it thus.

And now he had become a murderer.

18

After the first shot had been fired, Scholten wheeled around. He saw the Lieutenant sprawled on the ground, and his eyes searched for Albert Mutz. He stood there rigid as a statue, slightly bent, the carbine at his hip. His face looked old.

Good old Mutz, Scholten thought, as a wave of emotion surged up in him; a deep and tender affection for Mutz, who had proved himself a friend in every situation. He could have embraced him. But there was no time for that now.

Scholten had gone back to the bridge thinking that by merely brandishing his rifle he might prevent the demolition. That had turned out to be a fallacy. Still, the bridge had to be saved, he thought, or else what Mutz had done for him was meaningless.

"Scram," Scholten said to the men. "Go on and beat it, or there'll be more fireworks!"

"Pipe down," one of them said in a surly voice. "Can't you see we're leaving!"

Scholten and Mutz watched the five men return to their truck. It struck them only now that all five of them were unarmed.

"Now let's throw that junk into the river," Scholten said. "Then we'll be done and nothing more can happen."

He was only thinking of the demolition now, of the bridge, of the five dead comrades, of his friend Albert Mutz. He was not thinking of Hampel. And he couldn't know that these men had been with their Lieutenant since the beginning of the war, that they had traveled over half the globe together, building bridges and destroying bridges, and that more than once they had shared a last cigarette among them.

Nor did it occur to Ernst Scholten that they five might have left their carbines behind on the truck since they had no need of them at the job they were doing.

The men stood on the back of the truck, which started off slowly, crossed the rampart and disappeared from sight around the corner. Albert Mutz noticed that the motor did not drone off gradually in the distance, but that it had been choked off suddenly and was silent.

"Careful, Ernst!" he cautioned. "They haven't gone yet. They'll be back again!"

Ernst Scholten had taken hold of the first case and heaved it over the railing. I hope the damn things don't come apart and explode when they hit the water, he thought as he let go.

But all he heard was a hollow, swishing sound and already had a second case ready on the railing.

As he dumped the fourth case, he heard the first rifle shot whistle past his steel helmet. Ernst dived into the open shaft, and he saw that Mutz also was crouching inside the shaft on the other side of the bridge. Mutz propped his carbine on a case and stared over to the eastern bank.

I wonder if he's aware that the case is full of explosives, and what might happen if they put a slug in it.

But Albert was not aware of it at the moment. He was completely unaware of being in danger himself now. He only wanted to cover Scholten as long as he was dumping the cases into the river.

Scholten lifted another case out of the shaft, pushed it forward two feet to the edge of the bridge and sent it downward with a push under the railing. He repeated the process once more and was finished. At least on his side.

Again a few bullets came flying through the air. Scholten reached out a hand from the shaft and pulled his sten gun closer to himself. Then he disappeared again inside the shaft.

Mutz started to push the cases that were on his side off the bridge with the butt end of his rifle. The first one plunged down. Scholten stuck his head out of the shaft. "Hurry up," he screamed and disappeared again as another bullet whizzed past him.

Then he saw Mutz tug at the second case without making headway. I'll have to go over, Scholten thought. He needs me now.

He climbed cautiously out of the shaft, stood for a moment in a stoop, and felt a blow against his left shoulder that nearly toppled him. He took the sten gun in his right hand and staggered against the railing. He raised the rifle to his shoulder as best he could.

"This is it," he said to himself. "No more illusions now."

He saw the flash light up the eastern bank, and fired a shot himself almost in the same instant. He leaned the whole weight of his body against the hammering, rattling weapon.

He commanded his left arm to go up, to hold firm, but his arm would no longer obey, and hung limply down. Scholten gritted his teeth and fired again.

He heard a scream and was frantic with joy. He was no longer a soldier, he was playing Cowboys and Indians. He was Winnetou, the mighty chief. He had been hit in the left shoulder by someone over there; he'd kill the paleface.

Ernst Scholten grew sleepy. His finger was still on the trigger but the rifle was silent, the magazine was empty.

Where are the cowards? Scholten thought. Let them come so I can scalp them, all of them. He heard the motor of the truck start up, but it meant nothing to him now.

He thought: What is a truck doing here in the middle of the prairie? And then he thought: Where have I left my flute?

Albert Mutz had also heard the truck, and at the same time the rumble of tanks coming up from the west. They're coming, he thought, and no one will stop them now!

He looked over to Scholten and was frightened. Ernst Scholten leaned over the railing. His chin had sunk down to his breast and he looked as though he were asleep standing up.

He's tired, Mutz thought, and I'm tired too. Dear God, I can't say how tired I am!

He lined up the remaining cases at the edge of the bridge, and shoved them over one by one.

Then he went to his friend. "Come on, Ernst, we've done enough!" he said bitterly.

"We've defended the bridge, we've lost five friends, we've prevented the demolition and I—I have killed a man."

Mutz wept.

Suddenly he noticed that Ernst Scholten didn't move.

"Ernst!" He shook him. Ernst Scholten lifted his face and looked at Albert Mutz. It was the face of a dying man, only the eyes were still alive and staring with a strange glare. Scholten looked at Mutz, looked through him.

"I thank my white brother, he has saved my life," he whispered.

"Ernst," Mutz said imploringly. "Pull yourself together and don't talk nonsense. Tell me where you were hit. We must get away from here, the Americans are coming!"

"Americans?"

Scholten didn't understand him. Then he came suddenly to himself for a few moments. His eyes opened wider, he recognized Mutz. He tried to smile, but it turned into an ugly, grotesque grin.

"Albert," he whispered, "the bridge! Intact! You see? We've held it!" He seemed to be thinking, trying hard to concentrate.

"How was that again with the General? What was it, Albert, that he had . . . ?"

"It doesn't matter now," Albert Mutz said, and tears ran down his cheeks. "We've got to get away from here. That's all that matters now. Ernst, can you hear me? We must go!"

But Ernst Scholten's gaze had again strayed off into remote places. His face paled. Suddenly he opened his right hand, and Mutz saw that Scholten had all this while been holding the sten gun in his whitened fist.

The sten gun glided between the railings and Mutz waited for the splash when it hit the water. But the sound did not come.

Then he saw that the magazine had caught on the edge of the railing and that the sten gun was swinging to and fro.

As Mutz was about to bend down and pull the rifle up again, Ernst Scholten collapsed. Albert Mutz caught his friend in his arms and gently eased him to the ground.

Ernst Scholten's left foot pushed the rifle, and it finally plunged down.

Ernst Scholten lay on the stone slabs of the pavement, and Albert Mutz saw that his lips were moving. It looked as though Scholten were praying. Mutz bent down to the white face and held his ear close to his friend's lips. Ernst Scholten breathed heavily, and he tried to speak now, to shape words. He said: "Don't forget—don't forget—don't . . ." Then his mouth opened wide and red blood gushed out. He tried once again to breathe deeply, but suddenly his head fell over to one side. And lay still.

Very still.

Albert Mutz closed the wide-open, staring eyes. And Ernst Scholten lay there now as though he were sleeping. "Lord, be gracious to him," Mutz prayed. His lips moved mechanically and he did not think of what he prayed. His eyes were fixed on the face of his dead friend. The tanks were rapidly approaching.

19

For some minutes Albert Mutz knelt beside Ernst Scholten. His glance suddenly strayed towards the Lieutenant, who lay beside the pavement, and fastened on the pistol. The pistol lay next to the Lieutenant's outstretched hand, on the shiny wet asphalt of the road. The barrel of the pistol gave off a dull gleam; a piece of plastic covering was chipped off the butt. All this Albert Mutz noticed, so intensely was he staring at the weapon.

The pistol exercised a strange fascination on the motionless, kneeling boy. He rose, walked over, knelt down, and picked up the pistol. He took care not to come too close to the Lieutenant. He examined the pistol.

It would be over quickly, an inner voice tempted him. A sweet drowsiness came over him as he lifted the pistol high, stared into the barrel and put his finger on the trigger.

Slowly he curved the finger and felt a pricking sensation as he pulled the trigger further back.

He knew: Another millimeter, only the slightest pressure now, and it would be over.

Then he saw his mother before him.

He saw her sitting at the sewing machine, bent over her work. Then she lifted her face and looked at him. He heard her say: "You're so hard on things, Albert. I like to work for you, but couldn't you take better care of your things?"

And he saw his mother standing beside the bathtub and soaping his back. He saw her sitting on his sickbed that time when he had pneumonia and the doctors had given him up. His mother had never given him up.

The images blurred before his eyes, and Albert Mutz realized that he was weeping.

In disgust he threw the pistol away, went back once more to Ernst Scholten and looked at the lifeless white face. "Farewell, Ernst," he said, his voice choking. Then he heard the noise of the approaching tanks coming up from the west, heard the rumble of the heavy guns and a grinding and whistling in the air overhead.

The shells landed somewhere in the eastern part of the town, shrieked and then burst asunder with a muffled thud.

Albert Mutz left the bridge and walked up the road, keeping close to the houses on the left. He walked as one weary from long wandering who knows that the end of the journey cannot be far off. Two questions were pounding in his brain: Why did it come this way? What did it all mean?

He didn't know the answer—and yet, there had to be a purpose in life and even in death. When he thought of the bridge still standing, though it might have been blown up and its fragments at the bottom of the river, he had the feeling that there was a secret meaning behind it.

Not a very satisfactory one. But one that did exist. He, Albert Mutz, might never discover that meaning. But he would go on believing that it was there all the same.

As he walked up the road, he felt again how drained he was. He heard the thunder of the American artillery, the grinding of the grenades, the detonations. Once the air pressure hurled him against the wall of a house. Stumbling, he regained his balance and went on, feeling the wound in his arm bleed again. Stone splinters had eaten into his cheeks, and he felt his face burning.

He walked through this inferno of explosions—the rumble, the artillery flares, the thick smoke that came pouring down on the town—walked through this hell as though he were immune. He had no fear, no dread. He set one foot before another, as though it all happened elsewhere, far, far away from him.

He saw them again before him: Siegi Bernhard—how he had carried on the time they had put a bug in his shirt collar. Jürgen Borchart—super athlete, muscle boy, who couldn't bear to lose a contest. Karl Horber—the jolly show-off whose adolescent passion had to be satisfied by the perimeter of a peephole. Klaus Hager—with his inferiority complex and enthusiasm for music. Walter Forst—cynical, spoiled, pitiable Walter Forst . . . and Ernst Scholten.

Albert Mutz again felt the question pounding: Why? Why?

While hand-grenades exploded around him, while the roofs burned and walls crumbled, he asked as he walked on:

Why me?

And he asked further: What happens when one's dead? Does it end there? Is there any more after that?

He was frightened by his thoughts and prayed: "Forgive me, Lord, for having such thoughts."

In this way he walked on. In front of one house he saw a dented old car with a bright red cross painted on a white background. While the cannons from the west hurled death and destruction on the town, a door opened and two men came out carrying a woman. Albert Mutz ran up and held the door for them.

"The baby is early," one of the men whispered to Albert. "Must be the fright, but we'll make it."

The car drove off, making a way for itself through the debris, and disappeared. Albert Mutz felt that he was coming close to the meaning he was so desperately seeking, quite close . . . And a strange feeling of kinship with the two men and the unknown woman rose up in him. I hope they make it, he thought.

As he walked on he was aware that he had become calmer. The gnawing emptiness inside him had gone. He thought of his mother and of Traudl and felt a profound tenderness. They'd know how to shape their lives once this was over. Then he thought that he wasn't yet sixteen.

At last he came into his street. His carbine caught at the garden gate when he tried to enter. He took the rifle off his shoulder, looked at it a long time, then returned to the street. Grasping the barrel with both hands, he drove it so violently against the pavement that the butt end smashed.

Then he sat on the stoop in front of the house, put his elbows on his knees, propped his face against his hands. He sat there, staring into the night.

He didn't know how many hours had passed; he felt

something soft brushing against his legs. He took the cat on his lap and gently rubbed it behind the ears. Again and again his finger stroked the soft fur. From time to time he put his face close to the animal and, deeply moved, heard it purring.

The bombardment had ceased. As he heard the American tanks rumbling at the end of his street, he pressed the cat close to his face and walked to his door.

"High time for both of us to be home!" he said. Then he rang the bell.

His mother opened.

Before entering he turned around and looked back. The pale light of a new day dawned in the east.

*

I stood a long time on the bridge that evening. I looked down into the water. This time, too, I could find no answer to the question: What meaning lay behind all that had happened here? The traffic flooded past behind me, and below, the river rushed on. Its waters lapped around the sten gun that had been lying there these ten years. None of those who rode past in shiny new automobiles or on motorcycles, or who walked across the bridge in their holiday best knew anything about this sten gun. And if they knew?

An elderly man stood next to me. He didn't look at the river, but out to the road. He pointed to a group of young boys and girls racing past on motor scooters, and said: "The youth of today. Just look at them. This is what we've come to!"

I ought not to have replied, but my thoughts were still ten years back. I said: "The youth is neither good nor bad. It is like the time in which it lives."

And he, with paternal benevolence: "You're a bit young for such a judgment. You'll have to get some experience—you'll have to live first, young man!"

I gave him a long look.

Then I left the bridge.

ABOUT THE AUTHOR

MANFRED GREGOR was born in 1929 in a small southwest German town. He attended high school there until 1945, when, like the boys in his book, he was drafted into the "sixteen-year-olds," a group formed in a desperate effort to slow the Allied advance. "Coming out of that uninjured," he writes, "was quite a lasting experience for me. I returned to school with a completely new attitude."

After completing his university studies in 1948, he assumed the management of the foreign editorial department of a local newspaper, where he still works.

THE BRIDGE was written and rewritten seven times before he decided to submit it to a German publisher seeking new young authors. It was chosen the best of 400 manuscripts and published in 1958.